Summer of Seventy-Four

My Big Mistake

-

Daniel Adams

-

By the Pond

-

What a Silly Thing to Do

-

It's All About Martha

-

First Contact

-

What Did I do Wrong?

-

Summer Festival

-

Dan Becomes Himself

-

There's a Problem with Public Spaces

My Big Mistake

"Are you nervous, got a funny feeling in your belly?" Pa smirked, pushing my buttons but Ma had my back, always defending me the best she could.

"No, why should he?" She said boldly.

In her mind, I was doing what many rural, young men have done for years. The old Ford rumbled to a halt, dawn chorus calming as the sun topped the trees.

"We're a bit early. The bus will be here soon."

I wasn't interested in any of father's controlling comments, but he continued, "Remember, you only have an hour in Charlotte, and you'll need to eat something. Ma only packed a snack."

Why was he caring now?

"Leave the boy alone, he's nineteen," Ma chimed in.

"Well, I never went anywhere 'til twenty-three and certainly not all the way to Georgia," pausing, anxious, "Here it comes."

The bus labored, dragging my few things to the curb. It was going to be a long ride.

Pa wasn't giving up. "Now you be good."

Ma was getting irritated. "He's gonna be a farm hand. What kind of trouble you think he's gonna get into?"

"Yeah, learn how to be a farmer." Pa breaking normal personal distance, smelling stale clothes and breath sour from last night's intake.

"Unlike you," I murmured.

Before anything could happen, Ma pointed first at my father. "Now you leave him alone," redirecting her finger towards me. "John, get on the bus!"

With one foot on the step and a flash of my ticket the bus trundled on. Mother waved, back straight, seeming proud of me. The goodbye wave is expected but she meant it. She was going to miss me. Pa made his way back to the car, his single moment of compassion over.

I settled in a corner seat towards the back, stretched my legs and tried to close my eyes.

We lived north of Medford, the bus passing through on its way south. The town wasn't much; a lot of whites, some blacks, two churches, two stores, a gas station and plenty of farmhouses which looked like ours, needing work. The difference was their Daddies lost their job when the mill or mine closed, some in Vietnam, and not by the wayside.

There were a few larger houses in the heart of Medford, mostly Victorians also in need of help, relics from when the area prospered. The good times, before the depression era, were never resurrected with bigger, more profitable mines to develop. The wood mill was now part of a market, but since the boom of the 1920s my hometown had become a whisper, its fate cemented when highway planners didn't include an exit.

Medford disappeared, endless fields became a blur, bus at constant speed, each image roughly the same. If I shot my gun, the fields would become alive, pheasants rising from fledging corn, fluttering black silhouettes in the early morning sun.

My eyes, heavy, gave way to a splash painting of last night with Jessie disappearing, crying, screaming, "I'll get you, John Wesely."

Our little going away party didn't go well, starting with Jessie arriving late. I sat patiently by the window distracting myself by late spring, irises, wild jasmine and sprinklings of peach, pink and strawberry. Colors that remind me of her, wanting to spend as much time with her as possible, becoming impatient.

The white anxiety didn't appear, that day, Jessie's Oldsmobile appearing at the expected point, sliding down the one-track lane. I hid wanting her to think I was busy, and not waiting like a puppy for a treat.

Brass thumped oak, then another and another in rapid succession. The sound hit my stomach, contents oozing into my esophagus, gulping. Nervous, face flushed, I checked myself in the hall mirror. The shadow on my chin remained, only one hour since last shaven. No such thing as a sharp razor in this house. There was a photograph of Ma's two brothers after a game, thick dark eyebrows framing brown eyes, well built, handsome men, and I was proud to look like them. Many a night, especially when fourteen or fifteen I imagined being asked to play, my uncles throwing the ball, shouting, 'Come on John', their encouraging voices resonating in my head for years.

"You didn't see me coming. I'm used to being greeted."

Jessie was right being royalty in our community. Most guys would wait on the doorstep, salivating, but she was dating me and not any *other guy*. It was that philosophy that landed me with Jessie to begin with, being the only guy not to go after the golden girl. I wasn't interested because I didn't think there was a chance, not even a glimmer of hope. Then she decided to fuck with everyone's head and ask me out. How could I say no?

"I'm right here."

For an instant she looked delightful, radiating, expression quickly giving way to dissatisfaction. Aspirations for a perfect evening wilting right there and then.

"Ah, my tummy is sore." Jessie moaned, hoping she ate something bad but left her bag open, and had made a detour to the pharmacy, heart chopped, dreams dashed. She pushed her spongy lips on mine whispering. "We can still have a nice evening." A suggestive twinkle in her eye.

I smiled, relieved, kissing her, ushering her inside, kicking the front door shut. I looked at her closely, kissing her forehead and cheek delicately, hands following her curves to plump breasts bulging.

Sulking, "I was hoping to lay with you all night long, somehow."

Jessie's eyesight broke as she fumbled around my waist, hands momentarily on my butt, then inside my pockets, brushing against me, bringing a flash of desire creating multiple images of us together. She tossed her strawberry locks, and with piercing emerald eyes tauntingly said. "I see you were," dangling a square condom packet under my nose.

"Oh, honey!" She pushed me away, but I wasn't giving up, "It's our last night and I didn't know."

"We can do something later."

Thank god for something I thought.

"Maybe,"

Jessie teasing. Turning her head offering a perfect view of her sculptured face, "Right now, I'm starving."

Over dinner, I tried to be romantic with pleasant comments about everything Jessie but dried up pretty quickly.

"Stop looking at me. You're acting mighty creepy tonight," Jessie frowning.

"I'm just a guy who's gonna miss his gal," retorting.

"We've been going together for two years, never *once* mentioned matrimony, and now you're gonna miss me." Jessie, playing the forlorn chick.

"Of course, I'm gonna miss you." A statement said from need, declining to say anything more, preferring to use her image for brief fantasies. Her head at waist-level, where it should be, and not pointed to the sky like a Pre-Raphaelite dame. The time was slow, painful, for a charged man with countless desires, and I wasn't enjoying myself.

Trying to bring boyish charm to the situation we sat on the couch, wanting to see her smile again, and possibly, well yes. I chirped, quipped and acted like prince charming to no avail, Jessie holding her belly, in another world. I had to bring her back, my body telling me to.

Glibly, I uttered. "You know I love you."

The 'I love you' line is problematic at nineteen and predicated with 'you know' it's presumptuous, and a bad strategy even for a blow job but salacious thoughts misguided me forcing the stupid declaration.

Jessie gawped, seeing right through me. "Ah, crap. I'm the best looking in all of Medford. You guys are all the same."

I looked at her. "And?"

"Alright," she said spitefully. "You just want to fornicate."

"But we have…and …", stuttering, susceptible under pressure.

Emphatically, "I know what we have done."

I was getting nervous. My folks left the house for a few hours and time was running out, "Let's go upstairs," gently suggesting.

"No," Jessie quickly replied, "I hate your room, stinks of sweaty jock, wonder what you do up there?"

Her remark was embarrassing, even though the answer is never.

"Let's go for a stroll. The fresh air will make you feel better," I said optimistically. "I just want to make you feel better."

"Ah! That's sweet, you're not so bad, Johnny," Jessie tickling my chin, the only person whom I didn't mind using the diminutive.

I walked at her pace, stopping to enjoy long kisses, several motions of our lips pressing together.

"The fresh air making you feel better?"

She smiled.

Hitting the highway, the diesel engine got louder, bus reaching top speed. I felt safe, the world flying by, sixteen wheelers, sports cars, beaten-up trucks, and families on road trips. I was part of it, liberation felt great for an instant, but the scenery was dull and not enough to distract me from my problem.

I slid my arm over her shoulder, pulling her closer, giving her a quick peck on the cheek, not wanting to speak. It wasn't necessary, conflicting with urges rushing through my body, wanting her to caress me any way she could, and definitely not caring about her lady situation. I would have done it gladly, despite that, if given the chance.

Stopping, turning her around I forced my lips on hers, pushing her mouth open with my tongue. There was a patch of grass, taking her, almost falling to the ground.

Apart from, "Johnny what's you are up to," Jessie was initially fine with the idea, my hands and lips everywhere, becoming overly expectant.

"Calm down!" She commanded.

After spending nights not touching myself I was impatient and didn't want to control myself any longer. I am a boy. She is a girl. What am I missing?

Jessie wasn't just a girl, which is part of the problem, but a queen tiring of my random affection. No please, do not struggle; unbuckling my pants, ready, it had to me now.

We lay on the verge, awkwardly; my arm wrapped around her, "Common honey," whimpering like a little boy.

"Johnny you'll make me messy."

"No, I won't, I promise," pushing her hand towards the goal. She fumbled while I pushed my trousers down, my left arm remaining over her shoulder.

What made me say it is unclear, maybe that devil waiting in the wings, never using her mouth before, hands yes, grabbing her hair, while holding my phallus and angrily those mistaken, desperate words flowed out. "Do your job, for fuck's sake."

Jessie looked at me in surprise never seeing me as demanding, nor cursing, and I the fool was not done yet.

"Suck it, come on, suck it," pushing my cock onto her lips, her mouth not opening, squirming and trying to get away.

"Come on," hauling her back, grabbing her strawberry locks, Jessie squealing. I didn't care, really not minding seeing fear in her eyes.

"Do it... please." My cockhead prodded her face, Jessie gasped, eyes widened, freckles bunching on her cheeks, speechless. I tried to stare at her, my own eyes glazed over, was she or wasn't she going to suck it?

I should be tender loosening my grip. Jessie took advantage, the sting of her hand flashed over my cheek. She jumped up, shoe making a bee-line for my balls, reacting her leathered foot only landed in my belly.

"Get back here!" I shouted.

It was over, Jessie running down the lane, shouting, "I'll get you, John Wesely!"

Last night brought little sleep being frustrated, angry and humiliated. Exhaustion and the monotony of the diesel engine grinding pushed me over the edge.

***

Slumber was broken by horns, screeching breaks and sirens, stirring, awakening. Sun beating through the window, covered in sweat, chest-hair matted, light synthetic fabric sticking to my sturdy legs, needing to pee, my bulge embarrassing with zipper half down.

Across the aisle, a man smiled, anxiously correcting my dress. He wasn't in that seat before, remembering him sitting towards the front. He looked professorial with small, circular spectacles and a balding, shiny, sweaty head with a red tie hanging loosely around his neck. He pulled out a handkerchief, mopped his brow, gold wedding ring sparkling in the sunlight. He was older, smile kind. I broke the line of sight, not wanting to stare. 'Staring is pushing my business into yours', remembering Ma's word.

I sat up. There was no room in these so-called modern pants, regretting buying them, and not taking things into my own hands after Jessie ran away. It wasn't that easy, however, in fact impossible at home. If I made a noise Pa would say something. Same if I left a tissue in the trash. The shower was out since water was generally tight. The rule was army style for me, and if a pee or poop took more than two minutes it always encouraged a glance.

Pa was acutely aware his maturing son will want to masturbate and did everything possible to prevent it. It wasn't just him. This was how all fathers treated their son's in our small town. Ever since the age of eleven I've heard it wasn't God's will to spill seed. When first hearing that tripe I had no idea what the Pastor meant.

It's not like I haven't been down this road. I was thirteen, convinced in a safe place, downstairs in the basement. No one home, I thought. There was a small window. Somehow my father walked past and noticed my pants around my ankles. The door burst open, pulling his belt off, screaming, "I am going to beat the devil out of you."

Panicked I tried pulling up my britches. Pa said no, pushing me over his knee, taking the belt to my bare butt, letting out his self-righteous alcohol-fueled aggression, before throwing me off.

I stood in front of him, exhausted, humiliated, and vulnerable. If I had a few more seconds this would never have happened, Pa staring at the hanging stream of dew, then at his stained trouser leg.

I feared for my life as a full, swinging fist in my stomach. "You dirty, filthy pig."

Those words created a huge, fluorescent sign flashing every time I thought about it. Therefore, I never pleasured myself in my own house, and for that matter no boy from Medford did.

There was no discussion among us either, like solitary little creatures trying to defy nature's development. Still, we did it, all walking into the woods. If a boy met another on a trail, one turned to the left and the other to the right, no need to disturb. We were all in the same boat, adolescent dudes waiting on real pussy. I often wondered since we shared the same need, what if a buddy stood next to me. That would never happen. Stories told left them ostracized.

Building density increased, waited at traffic lights, watched ladies drag their kids and old men sitting on stoops, smoking, observing.

The older man across the row smiled once more before disembarking. I thought about his eyes surveying my body while I slept, not minding the intrusion *from him*, probably because he appeared fatherly and kind.

I thanked the bus driver for his efforts.

There was one focus, a bathroom, the ride to Charlotte taking all morning, spotting the sign I dashed over. The smell of urea hitting me like a brick wall. There were four spots

9

at the urinals, and three were occupied. Considering my condition I wasn't about to join them, taking the nearest cubicle.

I dropped my bags, unzipped, and gazed at the ceiling feeling urine well to overflow. Needing to go and erect is a problem, shooting in every direction like an uncontrollable firework, splashing the toilet seat wall and floor. I got the stream under control, the flow stopped, pausing for a second, not sure what to do. Should I clear up the mess? Desperately I grabbed something like parchment paper, smearing urine in an already very, dirty toilet, the stench overwhelming, trying to hold my breath. The plywood partitions between the cubicles deteriorated under constant vandalism, leaving a hole below the toilet-roll holder. The gap wasn't small and wasn't wishing to pry, a thick hairy thigh on the other side. Instinctively I looked away, offering my stall brother privacy, buckling my pants.

I headed to the sinks splashing cold water on my face, enjoying the brief fantasy of a real waterfall, my naked body bombarded by a mountain stream surrounded by luscious foliage. My head hovered, out of the corner of my eye, the same three men stood at the urinals, all watching me, leaving without drying my hands and face.

Where does the next bus leave from? There were dozens of buses in that dilapidated station, a rusty steel and broken glass structure about to fall on my head. I couldn't miss the bus as Mr. Adams said he'd pick me up. No phone in their farmhouse meant no way of fore-warning them if something went wrong.

I meandered, circling myself to confusion among all these people, signs, and hi-decibel, inaudible, loudspeaker announcements thumping in my ears. I found 37 but not 37E. None of the numbers ended in the letter 'E'.

In the crowd, perplexed, my head spun trying to locate a point of direction, anxiety building in my nerve fiber, synapses sparking like a sci-fi experiment with bolts of sapphire light.

I could ask at the ticket counter, but the queues were long, checking everything again, turning. This could not be possible. What would my father say when he finds out I missed the bus?

"Arrrggghhh," in maximum frustration, temples pulsating, pressure building, no longer seeing the world as others do.

"What's up son?" Behind a bus driver with his door open said after letting out passengers.

"I'm looking for 37E," shouting to counteract the noise around me, and the cacophony in my head.

"No E busses leave from here, son." He replied, making it sound like I'd have to walk miles, missing the bus without question. I was losing control. Panic fueled desperation dies before white anxiety rips, a nuclear explosion inside my fragile mind.

"What?... wherein God damn hell do they leave from?" My voice cracking, angry, and offensive to a working man trying to help.

The driver jumped out his seat, threatening, "Don't curse at me, son."

My mind crumbled, knees weakened, skeleton collapsing, too much confusion and mayhem to think. I wasn't used to seeing so many people, milling around, all thinking it's normal to bash each other with luggage.

My bags fell to the ground, arching my neck to the heavens yelling. "I'm sorry," eyes watering, tears burst, cheeks glistening.

The driver gesticulating advanced, "Calm down boy!"

He didn't understand the idea of fucking this up was terrifying. The driver's frame towered, an ogre looming as I cowered on cool concrete. In a teary blur, his body came closer, reaching down to assist in gathering this human mess together.

Helpless, my voice broken, "Thank you!"

His face was small and round set on a strong torso, muscles rippling holding my bags. His expression over a stubbled chin was more of amusement.

"E buses leave from the extension. In the new terminal... it's not far." The driver smiled like an older brother helping the family runt.

My shoulders dropped, head flopped forward, "Thank God."

With a sharp look and burning eyes, the bus driver pointed. "It's over yonder. Follow the yellow signs. Now get out of here."

His sharp yet sympathetic tone reminded me of my uncles as I ran from the scene, bags flying, not slowing until out the main station, looking back wanting to shake the driver's hand and thank him officially.

Less than a quarter-mile was a newer structure, and a whole new set of buses, in a partially finished project, the surrounding area under construction. My bus stop was easy to find with an adjacent concession stand to boot.

Correcting myself I addressed the driver with respect. "Sir, this the bus to Caravelle?"

"We stop there." The driver looked tired.

"Oh, thanks. Do I have time to get something to eat?"

"You bring smelly food on my bus and I'll throw you off." The driver clearly meaning what he said, throwing his body back in the seat, with a hand on the gear stick, I thought he was about to drive off.

I should have looked at the time and not bothered him. There were twelve minutes left, and no line at the concession stand, brats ready.

The vendor looked at me. Thinning blond-gingery hair stuck to his head, face alive from droplets of sweat and a beard days old. A mass of blond, chest-hair billowed over a stained, string vest surrounded by a soiled apron.

I pointed at a thick, semi-burnt sausage. "Everything." Watching him create my meal, spilling ketchup on this thumb, naturally licking it off like that was a waste.

"You got a soda?"

The vendor sighed. The effort to bend and fetch too much, pants dropping, the top of his buttocks covered in light ginger hair, darker whiffs flowing in his crack. Everyone in Baptist Medford looked perfect, pretended they were perfect, and it wasn't true. This man held his placard high, 'I am a poor man'. The contrast was evident, the world felt real, paying and thanking him. He said nothing, tiny polar-blue eyes drilling deep into my gut like pointed laser beams.

I ate the whole thing in a few bites, swigging cold soda, satisfied I'd made it this far. It would be a while before my destination and after almost an hour of excitement and cold pop considered my options. The need to urinate either imaginary or real is coupled with all anxious situations.

"Excuse me, is there a restroom?"

"Can't you see they're still building here? Back in the main station!" The vendor unhappy, probably at the commonality of the question.

"My bus is leaving soon, never mind," sounding needy.

He beckoned to come within whispering distance, leaning over the counter. "Go behind that wall, they're going to demolish it next week. All the guys use it for the time being."

"Got it!" Our vision clashed. He grinned and licked his lips.

I walked around. A man equipped with tool belt and safety helmet was finishing his business, packing himself away, giving a polite acknowledgment of my presence before disappearing to where the bulldozers and backhoes were busy.

I was letting out remaining waste when the vendor appeared being surprised to see him, instantly classifying him as someone I'd never see again. Instead of finding his own space, he stood remarkably close and to make things worse didn't seem shy. The vendor didn't unzipper, simply pulling out his dick as everyone else does, but pulled down his pants, penis and bulbous testicles hanging over restraining underwear. He smelled sour, of un-bathed flesh with an overtone of grill and fryer fat. This dude needs to buy boxers was my initial thought, as he pulled up his string T-shirt displaying a hairy belly and a blond-gingery bush. Why was he choosing to be indiscreet? He grinned, tip of his tongue stuck out of his sly mouth, expression was repulsive, but something made me do it and looked.

His foreskin extended over the top of his penis. Being circumcised it was intriguing, before wondering why the vendor hadn't started his business. The vendor had no business peeling back his foreskin, repeating the action.

The flow on my part, except for a few golden droplets stopped and couldn't look at him any longer diverting my gaze to what was in my right hand, trying to shake it like we all do. What happened was uncontrollable perhaps intoxicated by testosterone, my throat dried and blood pumped. It wasn't post-pee dick in my hand but my manhood, ready. I needed no reminding the bus was leaving soon, in a reactionary, survivalist manner, zippered and ran.

"You just made it." The bus driver said, immediately shutting the door, the deep rumble of the diesel engine following, making my way to the back. There could not have been more than fifteen people on the bus which suited me fine.

My mind celebrated, 'I didn't miss the bus', heart rate decreased. Being punctual is a part of anxiety, or is it anxiety means you're always punctual? I'm never quite sure.

The bus crawled through traffic. This was going to be long, slowly leaving Charlotte. The landscaped dulled from city to suburb, stopping twice, now the bus was almost full, then came the Interstate. The view of towns diminished into nothing but rural images flapping past my window like early examples of cinematography.

We were in the State of Georgia, new territory. My fellow passengers were a motley crew and beginning to annoy me. There was a lady with a couple of scruffy kids whom she struggled to control, miscellaneous elderly people, two nuns in long sweltering habits, one man with a teenage daughter, someone(s) that smelled and one very pretty girl. The girl and I appeared similar in age, immediately regretting not being more observant when getting on the bus, before remembering she got on afterward, wanting to sit closer and strike up a conversation. She sat five rows ahead, felt my stare, turning her head, long brown hair swishing over her shoulder. She did not choose to be coy, she simply was, letting out an inkling of a smile. I smiled back and broadly, briefly considering changing my seat. Public rejection in this small space made that impossible. No thanks to being emotionally naked in this long metal coffin when all eyes stared.

There were several hours to go, taking out the only book I bought with me, one of the few I owned. The thick volume 'Human Biology', was filled with layers of complicated text taking time to decipher, preferring to look at the sketches and templates showing actual photographs. My mother made a great effort to purchase it, opening it minded me she did everything she could.

I studied the pages or tried to; feeling pretentious as I am a farmhand. Secondly, I couldn't shake the vendor, how close he stood, openly fondling himself. The image lingered, fascinating me, never having seen, or should say, gazed at another man's penis before. At school the occasional chubby bounced around, however, eyes should be chest up.

I skimmed words using my interest in the subject as justification for intrigue. Of course, I was fascinated as he had a foreskin, it's biology, was one stupid thought. The scientific excuse didn't explain my brain independently flicking through Kodak shots of the head of his penis popping out when he pulled back the foreskin. A head larger than the curved shaft poking towards his belly button, plump testicles hanging low in a ball-sack mottled with blue veins. He stank, repulsive yet I was stimulated.

I glared out the window, fields turning into gently rolling hills, constant mesmerizing images forcing a sleepy trance. My neck muscles softened, head tilted to the glass, sweat droplets accumulating then running down my nose.

Thinking about Jessie would keep my mind where it should. The star of Medford who played violin, sung like an angel with three powerful, protective, even vicious brothers and a father who ruled with an iron fist.

To put Jessie into context, most guys, if they saw her naked picture would whip it out, offering a tribute in less than a minute.

Emotional rigor mortis set in after the event, now it waned, feelings of remorse attacking my heart, tiny primitive people with spears ravaging every ventricle. What have

I done? It was a pathetic boyish move. Why didn't I gently kiss her instead of becoming rampant? …replaying our going away party as it should have been.

We were chatting, cracking jokes, giggling. Jessie responding with another silly remark, laughing at anything and nothing. The first kisses would be simple brushes to her cheek like an artist adds accents of color to a canvas. I'd lower my tone, reminisce about our best moments followed by words of reconciliation before kissing her firmly, then gently, teasing her lips. Jessie waiting for me to guide her. I'd want to be become unpredictable: longer, slower, harder, each one increasing in intensity, my tongue making short trips into her mouth, smiling broadly before nestling in her bosom. Slowly Jessie would respond kissing me back and then I'd know she got all my messages.

She would feel me grow while kissing her for as long as I could, removing last moments of doubt. I'd bring her left hand over my buttocks, my groin meeting her palm. She'd see the urgency in my eyes, her fingers naturally grabbing my bulge.

She wouldn't complain and I wouldn't have to beg, eagerly undoing my zipper sliding her hand inside, massaging me. I'd have to help, flipping my top bottom, but she'd be the one pulling down my pants and amazed at what she finds.

I'd understand when she struggled with my girth, she was trying, spitting on it, only able to tease my cockhead. When the time came, she exclaims how much there was and not minding the mess.

If any of this happened my mind would be clear and not in this state. This was going to haunt me. I thought of her vengeful brothers led by their psychopathic father. There is one immediate resolution, food, the meaning of comfort.

I remembered the bus driver's words but the whole bus was filled with folks munching. Who will notice?

Ma made sacrifice after sacrifice, this was another, cracking open the tin foil revealing the piece of chicken missing from last night's dinner together with a biscuit. The air was quickly smothered by salty, fatty, fried skin aromas igniting appetites.

The bus became alive with chatter, folks turning their heads trying to identify the source. The bus driver complained, it was too late, all evidence gone, guilty party drifting into sleep.

***

The bus veered off the highway, down a ramp before stopping to enter the State route, jolting my head forward. The road meandered further South, cornfields, wheat fields, and orchards flanking a rolling landscape. Clusters of trees increased, hills rising higher and valleys descending deeper, giving hope this trip will be over soon.

This must be the town ahead. My stomach queezed at the thought of meeting Mr. Daniel Adams. I didn't know what to think, happily distracted by the outskirts. I'd find out soon enough.

Caravelle was at the intersection of State roads with an adjacent river. Farmers needed access to water, a store came, and then a church. At some point a big farming distributor moved in, meaning larger silos, trucks coming and going. Despite this, Caravelle would never have grown without small parts manufacturing. One of the small towns that made it. Water helps. My crummy town had none of this.

Daniel Adams

About a dozen of us got off. Others quickly met or walked away. The only one who lingered was me, which was fine being a process of elimination. Mr. Adams had the same idea and must be the tall man casually leaning on a pickup, gently waving. Approaching, he shot out a forthright hand, dropping my bags to return the gesture. He squeezed my hand too firmly.

"Daniel Adams, pleased you made it son."

His energy struck me, well dressed, smelling of carbolic soap.

"John Wesely…Hi…," thunderstruck, stuttering again.

Mr. Adams was animated. Eyes dancing observing everything.

"Here, let me share the load." One big hand swiped up my rucksack and sports bag throwing them in the back of a grey Ford, newer than expected. Hastily I followed.

Mr. Adams was taller by at least six inches, and I was too tall to be called stocky, that's for guys below 5ft 10'. His head was proportionally small compared to broad shoulders and the thickness of his neck, cleanly cropped, sandy-brown hair surrounding it. Dan glanced over, green flecks in his hazelnut eyes making me feel better. He was amicable.

The vehicle accelerated rapidly towards Benton some twenty miles south. The man had bravado, speeding, frequently weaving in the opposite lane. My eyes darted between the road and Mr. Adams, having one hand on the wheel teasing it just enough to create direction and an elbow out the window didn't have a worry in the world. He was casual and care-free, lips curling. "Trip all right then?"

"Yeah, too many people on the bus. How much longer?"

"Done your fair share of sitting I guess, less than a half an hour, promise," winking, pressing the accelerator.

Weren't we going fast enough? - looking at him in astonishment. His face was flat with a nose that went out a little too far before plunging down with lips thin above a pointy, peachy chin leading to an angular jawline.

"Yeah, you're right… I have… Got a square butt," laughing.

Mr. Adams was confident and for some reason the excessive speed wasn't scaring me, no physical reaction at all.

"We'll be keeping you busy boy. No square butts in my place, no doubt." We laughed as if this was the funniest thing in the world, feeling like I've known him forever.

It couldn't be much longer. Benton came and went, the farm being another five miles south.

"I'll show you around when we get there."

There wasn't any point in replying. Mr. Adams said what was going to happen, believing him with his friendly face inspiring trust.

We charged down a gravel road that only got narrower, catching each other's eye. Our smiles broadened seeming to understand each other.

Mr. Adams didn't de-accelerate before twisting the wheel. The pickup turned with little variation in speed, swerving around a seventy-degree angle, gravel kicking up leaving a dust cloud. The vehicle sliding, semi out of control amused him. It was also meant to excite me, and it did. That was cool!

The road's incline reduced the vehicle's speed, drifting along a two-tire track lane, grass in the middle, flanked by rows of peach trees, fruit forming in the sunlight.

Mr. Adams added. "See 'em, can't have enough of them, running out of space." He wasn't finished, "…and it's gonna be your job pickin 'em," sniggering.

My sense of trust diminished. The farmhouse lay ahead. The pickup crawled to reach the top of the incline as Mr. Adams now refused to apply gas. The topography declined the vehicle picking up pace before barely reaching the front door. He did this every time assuming Mrs. Adams wasn't in the car.

19

I remember Pa painting the exterior of our place. Now it peeled like bark on silver birch while Mr. Adams's farmhouse was well kept. The new paint attracted a yellow hue in the late afternoon sunlight. To the right, a deep red Dutch barn partially hid a chicken coup and garden. The curvaceous countryside reminded me of home. This could be our place. The difference was Mr. Adams.

"Common let's go," hopping out. "Grab your stuff now or later. I don't care."

I lunged, took the two pieces feeling the need to follow with no delay.

Dan flung the front door open. "Martha…we're here. She'll be in the kitchen," motioning to follow.

From a small vestibule we were in a living room with a dining area at the back, partially separated by a fireplace. The perfectly-polished, carved oak mantel was topped with framed photographs, one of a young lady with an apparent older and younger brother, and another of a handsome man in army uniform. Oak molding hugged the corners, and the fireplace made the room feel comforting, hardwood floors creaked. At the back was the kitchen with a big, cast iron stove, a wooden island and a pantry area stocked with cans and jams opposite a sink filled with dishes, pots, and pans.

Martha was busy re-arranging trays in the oven. Dan touched her on the shoulder pointing out our arrival.

"I see ya." Mrs. Adams straightening, chubby, round red face all screwed up, looking at me, softening but certainly no smile. "Okay then," grunting as if accepting something, a possible recurrence, before giving Dan a quizzing look.

"This is John." Mr. Adams said.

"Oh my! Of course, you are…," breaking off.

Mrs. Adams looked me over and I looked her over. She was short and curvy, small blue eyes, a button nose with rosy, turgid cheeks dominating her face and pinched lips struggling to hold even a modest smile.

"How do you do Mrs. Adams?" It was the politest thing I could think of.

"A bit of a bad time to be shakin' hands." Mrs. Adams dissatisfied started stirring her pot at an unnecessarily fast pace.

"Take the boy out the way, show him where he sleeps." Waiving her spoon indicating we were dismissed.

Mr. Adams didn't speak until we reached the top of the stairs. "Don't be worrying about Martha, she'll do you no harm. We surprised her a bit that's all, not been well of late."

It was awkward, a big man and a bigger man standing in an attic finished with two rooms, one larger than the other connected with a short hallway. Mr. Adams ushered me in, knowing there was little space for both of us.

The room was thin yet long, roof line inclining above a single bed, a small dresser with two items of decoration; a print in a gold frame and a vase. At the end a small window.

"Dump your stuff!" Dan ordered constructively, heading downstairs like a bull, beckoning at the base. "Come on."

When I reached the last step he was already outside, running to catch up.

"What we got here Mr. Adams?" Trying to be participatory, comment paying off, Mr. Adams turning, studying my body, face and smile.

"Not enough," stopping abruptly. He held out a strong arm, color of his skin paler when it met his shirt sleeve. He was long-boned, tri and biceps nonetheless filled the space between shoulder and elbow like a rolling hill.

"Pay attention!"

"Sorry, Mr. Adams." He looked at his arm, at me, creases between his eyebrows deepened wondering if there was something wrong.

"Call me Dan, Martha is Martha!" He exclaimed, "It's been irritating… *for everyone* so far!"

21

Dan didn't wait for an answer, he rarely did. "That's all peach." His index finger created a curve starting from the right, "Peach, pasture, corn", to some wooded hillocks before declining to two more orchards. "That's all apple."

The barn was double-sided, the front for equipment and apparently storing fruit with empty bushels stacked to the ceiling. Walking around the clean air was invaded by the smell of hay soaked in cow piss. There was a garden in various stages of development, bordered on one side by a hedge leading to a few acres of pasture, cows making themselves heard.

"We don't have many, sixteen right now, not trying to make myself a big herd." Dan paused, licking his lips, eyesight descending. "I'll sell a few in the fall."

The group masticated, occasionally swatting their tales while happily gazing into space. I envied them.

"Why aren't you trying to make yourself a herd?" I asked.

"Oh, cows are a lot of trouble, rather plant a few things and take chances with the weather. Built me a pond for additional water if mother-nature struggles," Dan pointing towards the wooded area. "Can't do nothing without water, in the meantime, this lot need milking."

Four cows could be milked at once, Dan sorted equipment. "Go get that one," reflecting, "No, start with that one, then the rest won't fuss." She was older, the matriarch, a thin cow with large udders kept for her reliability to produce a female calf.

 Dan paused, "Watch carefully, from now on you're doing this, sterilize first."

It was a simple apparatus of four sets of suckers, tubes, pumps and a portable storage tank, all newer, stainless-steel shining.

Dan crouched down and I did the same but didn't manage to see. The next one was easier, the noise increased, creatures either celebrating they were done or complaining they had to wait.

"Don't go too fast…they don't like it."

Dan explained the process, how to keep everything clean, more than I could absorb in one go, dreading forgetting details and forcing mistakes. Normally my stomach would revolt, not wanting to see his face when things went south, but his smiles and words of encouragement flowed like a never-ending stream of gold.

Dan unbent his lengthy torso and said. "Well, that about does it. Open the gate."

I ran, this not being the place to walk. The herd trotted towards the field, the eldest confused, Dan nudging her.

Dan's typical pace was fast, already way ahead, running to catch up trying to attract his attention.

"I think you might have to show me, one more time. We do everything by hand at home, only have a few," I said.

"That's alright son, not surprised, took me a few tries before I got the hang of it."

He had a kind face, one that accepts things and he was smart. Installing the new milking equipment was evidence of that.

"Hey," Dan said, with an eye of a father giving his son good advice. "You'd better get cleaned up before dinner. Martha is gonna want to smell soap."

"Where's the bathroom?"

He pointed. The bathroom was behind a sliding panel door off the dining room in a small addition at the rear that included the pantry, guessing it was the best place to put it, simply attaching it to the back of the house.

Martha liked cleanliness, disinfectant filling the air. I felt uncomfortable, wasn't home, stripping to my waist, washing in the basin.

I have to make it to my room, just up the stairs. I didn't hear anyone, sliding the door carefully. Dan stood one foot away, bare-chested, suspenders hanging from his pants. Taller than I, my gaze went to the funnel of fur from waistline to navel before multiplying into a forest of blond, his sweat contrasting with my freshly washed body. I paused, smelling, looked, all too long. He caught me, this the second time. I couldn't help it.

"I think it's my turn," voice deep. The warning of a man disturbed.

Embarrassed I scuttled to my room and found a clean shirt before going downstairs, hesitating at the sight of the laid table with a jug of ice-cold milk and aromas of bread and roasting meat. I wasn't sure where to go taking baby steps to the kitchen. Martha stood over a covered casserole, adjacent a loaf of bread cooling on a rack.

"Hello, Martha." She did not react in the first ten or even thirty seconds preferring to study my every move.

"Welcome Johnnie. My man needs help around here. We're gonna be pleased to have you," speaking under her breath but making her sentiment known. Likely semi-apologetic from initially appearing to confuse me for someone else.

"Thank you. Pleased to be here Maam," holding a respectful stance and steady eye.

"Here, make yourself useful. Put this on the table." Handing over an oval cast iron vessel, its weight surprising me, cloths slipping in my hands.

"Watch it, young man." Martha not about to let her food take a dive.

Dan rambled downstairs. "Take a seat boy."

"His name is Johnnie." Martha piped up.

"Prefer 'John' if you don't mind." It was my one and only request.

Martha took a seat opposite me, Dan at the head, lifting his hands, palms forward. Martha took his and I followed suit. I wasn't sure what he was saying, a rapid-fire inaudible blessing ending in a clear 'Amen.' Mr. and Mrs. Adams were Baptist with Martha appearing a little more 'Baptist' than Dan.

She was displeased at the blessing and its brevity, nonetheless, opened the casserole revealing a pot roast surrounded by potatoes and vegetables. The roast was dark, sticky on the outside and crumbled when sliced. Dan got up to distribute the food and saw my eyes on the meat, lips salivating, choosing to distract me.

"So… Johnny… tell us something about yourself." Dan amused at making me take the stand, but the caramel and spicy aromas of slow cooked beef was all I could think of.

"Oh," mesmerized. "I live on a farm."

Dan broke my line of thought. "I know that, you wouldn't be here otherwise. Happy to beat a smart ass, just lettin' ya know."

The broad appealing expression said he was joking. There is, however, an element of truth to every joke. It was clear that Dan controlled everything around him.

"Yes...no...sorry, but it's not like this one, not as nice," raising my voice to make my point. Dan backed off.

It was Martha's turn. "What do you mean?"

"Oh, it used to be, but things haven't been going that well." Thinking which reason to explain why, there were several. Dan stopped placing potatoes on each plate waiting for additional information.

"There have been a few dry spells then hit by a storm. The barn needs repairing," instantly feeling stupid. That wasn't going to be enough for a man like Dan who quickly replied.

"That happens all the time! You can mend the barn and work on water. Don't know what I would do without my pond." Dan predictably thinking my reasons pathetic.

"Yes, but Pa hasn't done that," I said.

My biggest problem is clarifying. "When it was me and Ma things were fine."

Curiously, Dan asked. "Where did he go, son?"

I had to let it slip, wanted to, seemed like information they needed to know, announcing. "State Penitentiary, came back when I was eleven, away for seven years." Now, this was too much information.

"I'm not asking what the man did, leave it at that," said Martha. Dan's expression disagreed.

"Still no reason not to keep the place up. He's been out eight years now, could have built it mighty and fine by now."

The food satisfied my appetite. Dan and Martha's appetite included more detail.

"Dad got into some debt, we lost twenty acres. Says he was swindled, since then things haven't been so good."

"Yep, that a problem!" Dan was smart commenting. "Sounds like the place ain't big enough to make it worthwhile."

Martha looked over her fork offering a sigh of sympathy.

They knew enough with the rest of the meal eaten mostly in silence. Dan's helping was plentiful but would have preferred to eat everything on the table, eyeing the remaining food. Dan saw my beady eyes and denied me. I didn't like it, even though expected, gluttony and Southern Baptist convention is a contradiction.

Martha cleared our plates, Dan pointing out church was at ten and there was work beforehand. It was awkward with only one choice.

"Haven't done a lot but feeling tired."

Martha had the last word. "Get out of here then."

The mattress was thin, springs squeaking when I rolled over. The roof line was the same at home, the bed marginally worse and food a whole lot better.

It was a long day, trying to let my mind go blank, never easy; a flash of Jessie, Dan bare-chested and the vendor. My hands caressed tummy hair, thoughts advancing to where the vendor was touching me while I reached back massaging his flabby pectorals.

It wouldn't take much before control is impossible, pulling both hands above the sheet, clamping the bedding over my body. It wasn't the first time, wasn't able to think about Jessie or imagining vagina close-ups all the time. Especially Jessie, couldn't think about her now after what happened. Maybe that's why I've reacted to the Vendor and Dan, desires now deflected to a different potential side of me, the other side of my brain. Wondering what's inside?

My thoughts deepened to Dan. The moment I set eyes on him my heart pounded. It was like shaking hands with a lion. Why on two occasions today, my first day, did I get caught looking at him in a way most men don't? The vendor was the catalyst.

If yesterday was bad, today in several ways was worse, being far from ready for a dissection of my sexuality.

***

Knuckles politely tapped my door, the suns first rays floating above my head. I headed to the bathroom; it was occupied, returning to my room, the sight of my bed to tempting, lying down. My body sent signals, a full bladder causing tension. It'll be fine after a pee and a cold shower.

Suddenly Dan was at the door. "Oh!" Startled.

He smiled brightly, hazel eyes filled with morning life, his sight at the center of my body. How could he not see it?

Dan smiled, "You'd better use the bathroom. See you downstairs." The fatherly comment was accurate.

I ran to the bathroom, slamming the door shut, embarrassed, swallowed by a strawberry flush. Dan chuckled in the other room while I peed like a girl.

Dan had bread and coffee, pointing at the offering.

"Eat up boy, then go and get those cows in. It's Sunday, never do too much on Sunday, animals always need looking after though."

The cows came without trouble, an easy set to handle. At home, they struggled even kicked, probably from discomfort. In a patient voice Dan set up the equipment explaining what to do again, before giving additional instructions on *his* idea of a clean barn.

"You know how to look after chickens I hope." He said cheekily, brushing my shoulder in a playful manner.

"Yes, I do, Sir." joking back. Of course, he got it, seeing it as confirmation of his dominance, that I wasn't going to give him any trouble. He liked that. The signs of approval were a junk adjustment and a smirk.

"Come back inside when you're done… there's more to do," giving me a cautionary look.

The barn was messy, cows like to defecate when milked, but not defied was soon in the chicken coop. This was easy. Sprinkling almost anything brings them out, collect the eggs, tidy up and refill water.

I took the eggs into the kitchen, passing Dan who sat at the table laid for a real breakfast. Martha was busy finishing a skillet of eggs and potatoes telling me to sit down. Like dinner, breakfast was plentiful. I just had the best two meals of my life, Dan noticing my appetite sliced extra bread. A change from last night and I didn't know why. Maybe bread is cheaper, and he still wanted to keep his boy strong.

Without looking up Dan said. "Don't know what time it is, but we'll be leaving at nine thirty."

Trying to be assertive "Can I walk around for a bit?"

"Yeah maybe," Dan replied. "Now I think about it, there's two milk jugs on the kitchen floor, go fill them. Oh!... wash and tray those eggs, put 'em all in the pickup. They're coming with us."

I looked at him quizzingly, he raised his eyebrows. "I said there was more to do." Dan saw this as questioning his authority and wasn't happy.

I filled the jugs, was washing shit off eggs in the pantry and could hear Dan in the bathroom behind, the sound of water, him grunting, water stopped. I was done wanting to get my stuff rushing past the bathroom door as it opened. The towel looked small, barely making it around his waist, his legs firm, except for a conforming belly he scarcely had any fat, my vision held by his skin, pink from scrubbing and Dan unconsciously grabbing himself to scratch. Startled I looked up, he grinned.

Before he could say it, I did. "My turn, thanks… smart you said… coming right up," beaming a defense smile, Dan laughing.

I didn't feel too bad this time. Don't men admire each other's physiques?...guys like to work-out and they look at each other's bodies. Anyway, he's just a man coming out of the bathroom, something I wasn't entirely used to, quite like that. My Pa was very shy, his stomach bulged, had a stubbly chin and little muscle definition. Dan smelled of soap whereas Pa smelled of sweat, tobacco, and alcohol most of the time. I wish I had a brother.

***

'Bethlehem Baptist' was a small, white-washed, church with a one-story addition hanging off the side used for community space. A bank of trees flanked the far side which bordered the property, parking lot almost full. Pre-church groups stood outside interspersed with kids, some with that awkward adolescent gait, the youngest chasing each other.

Dan gave orders. "Hey boy, see that side door," directing me to the community space. "Take the eggs 'n' milk and bring 'em inside."

My arms were full. Someone must have seen me, the door flung open, a young female smiling. "And who might you be?"

Her hair was brown, tied back, with a freckled face that I didn't find pretty, and a crisp fitted dress showing curves.

"John," taken aback.

"That doesn't tell us who you are," said a different head popping up behind, equally unattractive.

"Work for Mr. Adams," hesitating.

"We know that! You wouldn't have eggs and milk otherwise. You're not very good at answering questions, are you?"

I was stunned, these girls were confusing me, but Martha was already there.

"This is John everyone! Mary Beth, Mary Ann, you be nice to this young man."

"Yes, Mrs. Adams." The two girls making a synchronized half-curtsy.

***

The minister droned, his words not reaching me, never did. My reaction always the same. You have to be joking! My eyes wondered, playing the congregation game, making up lives and stories about the visually interesting. Firstly, I separated the kind faces from the severe. Mary Beth and her family certainly belonged to the latter category, as did Mary Ann's. Others were possible candidates including a family who sat one pew ahead. His wife admired him, he admired her, exchanging glances every time the Pastor said something relevant, enjoying one religious moment after the after. It wasn't only religion that made them smile, they were a happy, content couple. The children evidence of that.

The father immediately reminded me of a younger version of the professorial man I saw on the bus; tall, proportionally built, baldness encroaching on thin blond hair. He even wore the same spectacles and had the same genial expression. His wife must have been in her early thirties and very pretty, hair perfectly done, brown locks bouncing on her shoulder's, a country version of Jackie O. I'd also be a very happy man if I was married to her, I thought.

One of the kids must be from different blood. There were two of the girls that played outside and an odd man out, a lanky carrot-top who was more interested in me than the Pastor. He looked definitively, using the polite expression for staring. Not ready to catch his eye I looked at the Pastor. The boy still had eyes on me, feeling them, irritating me. When I looked back, he instantly looked at the cross which continued, on and off, until the Pastor finished his service.

Trailing Dan and Martha we slowly exited, the aisle jammed with people all seeking light and fresh air.

The churchyard was rife with chatter. Some folks exchanged pleasantries while others formed groups separated by sex, who engaged in serious conversation. Dan told me to stay with Martha walking over to the family with the pretty wife. Again, the red-headed boy stared, irises bright aquamarine eyes, every time I turned to check on Martha. Her rosy cheeks were fading, coordination off.

"Martha!" Making sure she had my arm for support, her body shaking slightly, breathes deepening. Out the corner of his eye, Dan noticed, rushing over.

"Come on let's get you home," clutching her arm. "Hardly surprising, darn church is stuffy. Never worked out why they have to keep the doors shut."

Dan drove at a reasonable speed. In the side mirror a car was trailing us, same family, a flash of red bopping in the back seat.

Martha ghostly and breathless went upstairs immediately leaving Dan despondent. I felt sorry for him, the carefree man from yesterday had disappeared.

"Let's get some lunch," Dan suggested.

We found the leftovers from last night, some bread, and ate in practical silence, focusing on our food. I thought did Dan have a premonition last night, that we'd need this food savoring every last bit.

"I'm running a few errands this week. It's gonna be a lot of work for you," sighing, remaining energy leaving his body. "You might as well enjoy the afternoon. The only time you'll have 'til next Sunday."

***

I didn't want to stay in that small room, surveying the landscape. The peach orchards were predominately between the road and a parallel that included the farmhouse and the barn to the right or North. There was another out-building, the other way, down the hill, a deteriorating barn surrounded by un-kept apple trees. Behind the orchards the topography rose to a long pocket of woods cresting the landscape. Instinct told me that's where I need to go and put my head down, kicking up dust, heat beating losing my shirt, clear sweat gems congregating.

The woods were a mix of trees and shrubs; oak, beech, buckeye, and hickory with a worn path. They were not that wide, fifteen minutes at my pace before more fields and orchards. On the other side was another farmhouse, a large barn identical to Dan's, and another dilapidated outbuilding.

I used the woods length to stay out of sight, traversing the small hill, following the descending ridge. In the middle ran a small stream with intermittent baby waterfalls, the sound creating instant relaxation. A sound I could focus on, always leading me from worry. All of nature's sounds are antidotes to life problems, even nature's colors work. In a bet I could think of twenty shades of greens or blues.

What I wanted was a soft patch of grass, to dwell, take a nap, a place where all I hear was nature and if possible be part of nature. A place where I had some privacy and the ability to see if someone was coming. The covered ground next to a large oak was mostly moss and fern kicking off my pants, bundling my clothing for a pillow, speckled sunlight beginning to warm my body.

I knew what I wanted. There's always the moment when you check yourself, in my case huge florescent signs flashed. The guilt never lasts, quickly beaten by human necessity.

My hand wandered, fondling myself over cotton shorts, reminding myself images of touching men will disappear when this is over. It was all due to frustration, regretting Jessie not doing it, regretted what I did, and now I had to.

I closed my eyes slipping my hand underneath the cloth feeling my girth. One fantasy was me and two girls. It wasn't a fantasy that I'd chosen, but one Medford boys talked it about all the time. For a long time thought if I didn't think about anything else, I wasn't normal. At fifteen the idea of another dude doing the same thing started. At seventeen I was going with Jessie feeling obligated to jerk off to Jessie doing things she'd never do.

Now I was left with a choice and a mural of intertwined bodies unfolded, men and women elegantly interacting. Two women fondled each other, one woman on her knees before three men, two men inside one woman while the third licked her clitoris. This is where I wanted to be, a place of freedom, from thought, and restrained preconceived ideas. The world I had in my head was different.

The process was going to be quick stopping to tease my balls, flicking them, liking the sensitive area underneath. My fingers traveled the hairy path, index finger gently dabbing the outside. It was moist, sweaty, a sweet yet pungent smell, olfactory opium. My right hand grasped harder, enjoying longer strokes, spitting, smothering the head with saliva. I opened my eyes, my penis glistened, head a deep red, squeezing a globule of clear sticky liquid, wiping it off savoring the salty taste.

The breeze picked up, leaves rustled, a bird let out a sharp squawk. My left-hand tugged on my scrotum trying to bring down tight balls. I picked up another gear, twisting, activating every nerve. From deep within the sensation began, pulling my hand away, my chest heaving sucking in air.

Moaning, focusing and waiting on nature to take over, the need for fantasy gone, not hearing the stream, nothing, masturbating in slow, soft stokes. That feeling from deep within returned with increased intensity, harder to stop this time. The sensation rose barely able to bring it under control, the first part appearing as one thick, white worm.

I like my sperm, seeing it as power. To a woman the possibility of carrying my baby and to man a weapon, smearing it around my frenulum, lightly stimulating it, enough to push me over the edge, gripping under the head letting the euphoric sensation build and build. Semen traveled, faster and faster, it was my job to fend it off. The fluid backed up, endorphins pumped, feeling it in the whole of my body. I could no longer shooting a thick white stream dancing in slow motion like the perfect ballerina. Another swelled squirting on my chest, then another, until the flow slowed to droplets accumulating on my dark pubic hair. I felt dizzy, my brain thumping coming down from an extreme high, squeezing the head again pushing out every drop.

Wow! All that shit is out of me, flinging my head back, breathing deeply to replenish my blood with oxygen. Time had stopped, and the world disappeared. Never for long enough, of course.

The sounds of the woods returned, the small waterfall and the stream. A chipmunk was busy making chipmunk sounds, either happy with himself or trying to warn others of impending danger scurrying up and down a tree trunk.

My head jolted forward as a nearby bush rustled, a crack of a stick, then another, something or someone was moving. I could not be certain, the sunlight causing a contrast with the shadows. Was that a flash of ginger bolting through the foliage?

Frantically I grabbed leaves discarding my life to die on the ground, always having the same thought. That wasn't important scared at the possibility of being observed. No, please no, initially dispelling the fact, but it had to have been the red-headed boy from church.

***

I learned my jobs, there were many, Dan jobs and Martha jobs. Martha took me aside while cleaning pots, questioning me about everything. I acted dumb when she went too far. This is the first line of defense for anyone who does not know; pretend to be naïve. If a predatory evangelist asks you to go to Sunday school, tell them you go to school Monday to Friday already.

After a thorough examination of all facts Martha remained concerned for some unknown reason. I couldn't say anything, then she shrugged, "I'm sure it will all work out," sucking in oxygen, "and don't forget his paper," frowning.

It was the hoarse voice that forced me to send her upstairs and report the incident to Dan.

That week, Dan and Martha disappeared for a day. When they came home, Martha was ghostly, Dan stressed. The next few days we tended things the best we could. It crossed my mind Martha's illness might save me from going to church that Sunday and the possibility of seeing that boy. I was wrong.

***

The same congregation was present, mostly, the ginger-haired boy sat in the same place. Being polite I acknowledged him. He nodded back adding a wry smile. Now convinced it was him in the woods, angry, the ginger dude broke bro rules. How long had been looking, what had he seen?

The Pastor rolled in and out of scriptures interspersed with personal words of wisdom, the power of love, anger, and forgiveness. I hated his words had relevance in my life, why was the sermon tailor made for me? Equally irritating were the numerous smirks and grins from ginger boy. His audacity made me want to drag him from the chapel and beat him. The Pastor finished asking everyone to pray for Martha's good health and quick return.

Dan broke away from three fellow farmers walking towards the same family, calling me over, ginger-haired boy trying to hide behind his assumed family members.

"Hey these are our neighbors…This is Mr. Stenton." Dan laying out an arm presenting the remainder of his family.

Dan ordered, "Say hello to Simon. He's helping Mr. Stenton this summer."

Hearing his name, the boy jostled his way to the front.

"I'm Simon."

His hand was limp and crushing his puny phalanges was pleasurable. Simon looked down as I increased the pressure, eyes wincing accepting the pain without complaint.

"John," I said but my eyes read, 'if we weren't in a churchyard, I'd be pummeling ya'.

"Yeah I know." Simon forced his hand away, but I wasn't done.

"Why you been looking at me all funny?"

He was younger, probably only a year, with a heart shaped face surrounded by shaggy ginger hair, reminding me of one the little dudes who carried Mary up to heaven, except they are fat, and he was thin. Simon scraped his souls submissively on the dirt.

"Don't know," is all he could muster.

There was no eye contact and knew it was a lie.

Dan appeared done and I knew better than to keep him waiting. With a sharp eye and my index finger pointed said. "I will see you again."

On our way back Dan struck up conversation with another man, broad shouldered, mostly bald with sides of dark cropped hair. These were two people who knew each other well, sometimes it's obvious, chatting, joking and slapping each other on the back. I walked past wanting to mind my own business and should be waiting by the pickup anyway. I felt eyes on my back, instinctively turning. Not just any eyes, not Simon's eyes which were inquisitive, but eyes that had no good in them, feeling cold. Planted on the man's chest was a badge.

The Sherriff and Dan were big men, his friend broader but shorter, a person who made a concerted effort to collect extra muscle. Should I have stopped to say something? No. Simon irritated me breaking a rule, bothering me in the woods. My mind was fixated on Simon and not paying attention to the Sherriff and it should have been.

My eyes were on the road, best place for them when Dan was driving.

Dan smiled, "So you met Simon."

"Yeah." My face grimaced.

"Hey boy, I want you to be friendly to that young man."

He'd regret saying that, in the meantime I thought, maybe after I beat the little fucker-up.

The pickup took forks in the road. I hadn't taken this route many times but knew enough to realize something was different. Dan took a hard turn, the road a dirt trail, almost non-existent, overgrown, at the end was the same old barn I'd seen from the farmhouse. The apple trees grew higher than the barn itself, a semi-secluded and idyllic space.

"What we are doing here?" Instantly my imagination wondering. The place was idyllic and quiet, a place away from anywhere else and that its problem, my mind going into a rabbit hole.

"I need a part." Dan looked blankly, impassioned, the skepticism of entering the barn with a man who could overcome me by force momentarily leaving me.

I pressed the subject. "What are we looking for?"

"A large bolt... should be one on the old tractor."

The barn was cluttered with old stuff; tools, a bicycle, furniture, signs, and a tractor. I fear such places. In our world, barns are scenes for bad things looking at an old mattress with dark stains.

Dan pulled the bolt from the back of the old tractor. I headed for the door not standing to be in this place any longer.

"Hey, John, wait a minute."

Chills ran down my back, starting to shake wanting to get out, slowly turning. Dan was a few inches from my face, breath on my cheek, long arms wrapping around me. He squeezed tightly, slightly lifting me off the ground, swaying, instinctively burying my face in his shoulder, his hands rushing up my back.

36

"What's wrong buddy," hugging tighter. "Are you sick?"

I didn't answer, his hands teased the muscles around my neck forgetting where I was. His energy swept through me like a cure for illness. Not like, it was the cure, magical, a human version of all of nature's sounds and colors multiplied by a million. For an instant I was free.

"Go have fun this afternoon."

I liked his command.

"You been to the pond yet, mighty fine day for a swim."

By the Pond

It was fair sized, more than a quart an acre, doing lengths back and forth like a robot, gasping for breath. It wasn't enough, needing to expel every drop of frustration doing push and sit-ups on the verge, crashing only when my muscles revolted, sending waves of pain greater than those in my head.

The feeling after a work-out is always the same, mind blank, blood flows adjusting, relaxation. I didn't want to think about it, my body told me too, and it wasn't for long.

The small chill wasn't from a breeze but from the feeling I wasn't alone. A foot cracked a stick, an unmistakable alarm, out the corner of my eye a pair of scrawny pink legs were in view.

"What the fuck, you doin' here?" I said.

"Mr. Stenton's property line is exactly in the middle of the woods and he owns half this pond. I have as much right to be here as you," his finger drawing an invisible property line. Simon was a cocky fuck but in fact never wrong.

"Mind if I join you?"

"Doesn't sound like I have a choice."

Simon was already taking off his clothes. He had a few, hard to see hairs on his calves and half thigh traditional undergarments, baggy around his crotch. The dude had no junk, chest hairless except for a pink mirage floating over his skin. Uncomfortable pulling down his underwear in front of me, he turned. I assessed this crime of a body, muscles so spindly they could barely lift a hay bale, reminding me more of a girl. He tried to yank them off only getting stuck around his ankles, forcing him to bend over. He shot me another glance to make sure I wasn't looking. Of course, I was, this is comedic. His underwear had a slit at the back, so he could shit without taking them off, chuckling.

"What so funny?"

"Ah nothing, maybe because it's Sunday."

Dan said I should be friendly, and I will, maybe. In the meantime, it was going to kill me talking to this boy.

"Mr. Adams working you pretty good to then?" Simon asked.

It was easier to nod.

"Me too." Simon realizing, I wasn't the friendliest, laying his body too close to mine.

"There's not a lot on ya."

I shifted a little, his ribs showed, stomach concave led to a red bush and a thin penis, foreskin extending over his glans reminding of the vendor. What's up with these ginger boys and their uncut dicks?

"I do Okay. Mr. Stenton said I'm doing a fine job."

"Really, he gives a reward or something?" I said sarcastically. His response is why sarcasm is never a good idea.

"Well yes! Every week I do a fine job I get an extra dollar or two." Simon said boastfully.

This statement angered me as Dan gave squat. Why was this puny, pink punk reaping rewards when I wasn't?

"You're a liar. We get nothing."

"You get nothing. I do!" Simon said in a convincing manner, my temperature rising. I was being screwed, skin turning red, blood rushing into my flesh.

"Bet ya can't prove it," my tone 3rd grade.

Simon crawled to his pants like a big, pink lizard, then to my astonishment peeled back three dollar bills.

"Didn't get my bonus the first week but done good since."

Blood welled again, waves of heat, this was jealousy. Simon again flunked his body too close to mine making the decision not to let this go.

"Move away from me. What are you… a fag?"

"I ain't no fag."

I heard this as a lie. Straight guys don't blush at the accusation and guys don't spy on each other in the woods. Now is the time to confront him.

"Yeah, but you hang around in the woods watching dudes jerk off." Moving my body to a dominant position, his thin body laying below, wanting to take him and spit out the pieces right there and then.

Despite Dan's wishes I couldn't like this guy. The antipathy of what masculinity should be, his body, lack of hair, unremarkable genitals and a little pink ass hole, all feminine. Where I come from this is meat.

Simon was initially silent then timidly spoke. "I didn't mean too. I was walking."

This irritated me. It's against protocol, needing to teach this jerk some rules, jumping on his chest, my thighs straddling him, dick flopping between his rosy nipples.

"But you don't spy. Why you spying? You like dick?" My meat grinded on his chest, "I think you like dick."

"No… please no… just never seen that before."

"What you never seen before?" Anger evident, an animal about to attack.

"Well, you know." Simon eyes couldn't catch mine, naturally going down to meet my pee and cum hole.

I pushed my penis towards his mouth, Simon swiping it away. The dick slap hurt, making me want to teach this bitch a bigger lesson.

"I know you want to, ya wouldn't be spying otherwise. Here's a real piece of the real action," wavering my phallus under his nose.

I wasn't sure what he was doing with his arms, turning, Simon grappling with his reptilian penis.

"You jerking boy. Stop touching yourself?"

"I was scratching."

"You're a liar like you were with those three dollars."

I didn't care if Mr. Stenton had given him the money for hard work, in fact I was happy for him, but it was his cheeky mouth that pissed me off and I was thinking about filling it. Maybe it would stop him gurgling shit is what my teenage mind said, rubbing myself under his nostrils. He needed to know what a man smells like.

I initially thought I've never done this before, then remembered what happened the night before I left, justifying these actions as different…this was a guy. Eventually random rationalizing informed me that if I fucked-up, like spying on a bro, this is the lesson I'd receive, violence being the only form of conflict resolution I knew.

"You see, you're not saying no."

I dick slapped his face a few times. Simon's body squirming beneath me, tightening my knees so he'd couldn't move.

"Get off me." His little fists beat on my abs like a pussy cat walking across my chest.

"What the fuck you gonna do about it?" I challenged.

"Listen, I didn't mean to look, sorry." Simon's face arching away from my cock head.

"No, get your face back here, you need a lesson. When we are done you will never bother me, or any other bro in the woods, ever again."

Simon looked stunned at the prospect of me making him suck me off.

"You understand, this is what happens to guys who watch," wanting confirmation. Simon was silent, impatiently giving him a quick slap.

"Yes." Startled, his light blue eyes sparkling like jewels in the sun light making him oddly attractive. His answer, however, was insufficient.

I grabbed his hair. "Open your mouth."

Simon gaped his tongue out and I used his brittle taste buds to tease my turgidity.

"Come on buddy."

Simon's eyes were wide open. He liked the fact I called him buddy even though at this stage he was far from it. He spat, massaged my shaft then squeezed his eyes shut before opening his mouth wider, engulfing what he could, one slow stroke at a time.

"Keep it up, don't stop," reaching deeper into his mouth. Maybe this is what I wanted to do to Jessie, now playing out my sexual fantasy with a boy.

Simon was fine with it, enough… kinda… not, eyes bulging when I went deeper, making me harder. I moved in an out, my climax mounting, his lips clenching, throat opening, each stroke good as real pussy. He gurgled, struggling to hold out, but I wasn't going to stop, not at this point.

Over-anxious I thrusted, Simon's teeth grazing my cock pulling out, but I was almost there, Simon noticing it. His mouth didn't clam up, as a non-compliant would do, instead, he stuck out his tongue like baby bird waiting to be fed.

I jacked it, nothing else to do, but hadn't forgiven Simon wanting to humiliate him with deep shots down his throat while holding the fuckers nose. Instead, it spewed mostly without control, managing a shot in his mouth and a couple in his eyes. That should teach the little fucker.

 I felt guilty the moment I was done. Simon's eyes were stinging, screaming, a shrill, letting him go. Blind, on all fours, Simon crawled down the embankment, splashing his face while gargling with pond water. His heaving chest froze, face turned, ginger hair matted, mud on his shoulder, grimacing.

"Why the … did you do that?" Simon aghast, presuming he wanted to swear but restrained himself. In fact, a cuss word never came out of his mouth.

***

The day I arrived Martha buzzed around the kitchen and with few exceptions hadn't seen that since. Tonight, was different. She made a thick soup of beans, potatoes, and lumps of pork. We ate in silence. Dan stared at Martha, her strength witling away, sorrow welling in his eyes. She tried to look back, her expression showed no emotion, face vacant.

"Common let's get you upstairs," Dan needing all his strength to support her. Together they made it up, certain that hadn't been always the case.

I felt guilty even though had nothing to do with it, clearing the bowls. Dan and I were hungry. The only wasted food in Martha's bowl, half full.

Dan came downstairs, convivial considering the circumstances, smiling. "Thanks, son."

New to the house, it was difficult to say anything, not able to inquire about Martha, she was ill and that is all I need to know. Confused, troubled I wanted to scram preferably to the woods but started to my small attic room.

"You've forgotten my paper."

I was told this irritated him, however, the sprint made me feel better.

Dan relaxed in his chair; a glass of amber liquid next to him. I unwrapped the paper presenting it as if a Christmas gift.

"Sit down," Dan commanded proceeding with a long list of jobs combined with do's and don'ts. It was his way of saying don't forget the paper.

The next morning Martha was not in the kitchen, nor at lunch or at dinner, only Dan and I thumbling around. Dan said little while we worked, worried, the strain making him snap on occasion.

***

It was in the middle of the fourth week when Dan and Martha left before sunrise, engine rumble jolting me from a dream. Jessie and I were married and have twins who scream the whole time. Jessie is nowhere to be seen. Once I changed one diaper, the other takes a crap. There are no diapers left and now the sheets are dirty.

I started shortly afterward sorting the cows, cleaned the barn and then to the coup. Dan's instructions included cutting grass along the lane, pluck and weed the garden and how to pick correctly, detailing what the market saw as perfect fruit. Last night he stated never wanting to see a peach or apple on the ground. It was my job to make sure that never happened. Today is the first day of harvest.

The day was long; the number of trees that needed inspection seemed exponential. From each tree only a few could be picked, at the edge of the orchards there were more. The day wore on, bushels accumulated on the trailer, muscles flexed, sweat poured off my body, underwear stuck, and my anus itched. The many scratches on my arms stung, results of mishaps a novice picker experienced.

Hungry and thirsty I went to the kitchen sink, turning on the faucet burying my head in cool heaven. I found bread, savagely biting off hunks, drinking more water, the bread getting stuck in my dusty throat.

The sun descended, below three quarters in the sky with no sign of Dan and Martha. I sat and pondered, quietly congratulating myself on an impressive bunch of bushels, hopefully even by Dan's standards. Then the lightning bolt struck, the paper, the damn paper. They could be home any minute racing to the post box, blindly pulled out the newspaper barely noticing a letter falling to the ground. I was three steps up the lane before turning to pick it up. The letter was addressed to me, recognizing my mother's haphazard handwriting instantly.

John,

Did you have a good trip? It's important I write.

It's not been long since you left. The moment we got home, Jessie's Dad and brothers came looking for you. I told them you were on your way to Georgia. None of them would tell me what's going on, man's business. They asked to speak to Pa, and I told them he wasn't around but then he rolled up. Pa was angry, and I went up to see what was going on. They said you disrespected Jessie. She spent the whole night crying. I wasn't sure what they meant, that's not like you, bad words were spoken. I hope that's not true son. You young folks were supposed to have nice evening together.

It's bad John, they're gonna take it out on you, true as God is alive. Write Jessie and say sorry, soon like. Jessie likes you just fine so make it good.

Tying to help you son. Don't tell your father I ever wrote you.

Love Ma.

My heart sank, knees felt weak. Flummoxed I sat and re-read my mother's letter. What have I done? It really was this bad. Jessie's family was righteous and would make this wrong right in their sick minds, an array of possibilities appearing, one more horrific than the other.

There was no shortage of 'an eye for an eye and a tooth for a tooth' stories, all taking place in out-buildings, away from others where it's easier to clean the mess. These folks like to match their revenge with the crime, and what I did was sexual. There were stories to scare the youthful male from going too far. Would they, as rumor suggested strip me, gut-punch me before leaving me in the woods to suffer the humiliation of walking home naked, dirty and bloodied? I hoped so, other stories were much worse, since it's not uncommon in our culture to deal with offenders with the very same offense except perpetrated by members of your sex. They would think nothing of raping me. It wouldn't be their first time and not the last.

I buried my head in my knees, fearful of the future and returning home, more vicious images racing of their various ways and means. Please give me a straight-up beating. I shook my head trying to focus on the scenery, the rolling hills, the sun as it slowly disappeared, the world was a beautiful place. If Jessie doesn't accept my apology, I couldn't go home and would have to see this big beautiful world after all. I was gonna miss Ma, shaking, horror still circulating.

The cows filed into the barn in an orderly manner. They were obedient, hard to understand why Dan didn't like them.

I couldn't think about Jessie anymore, she was upsetting. This was the first time my gut squirted acid since I got here.

The cure was Dan wondering how old he was. Martha looked early sixties while Dan early fifties. The photo of the young man in army uniform, on the mantle, had to be him, guessing he was tied up in Korea.

There were guys from home, that went to war, either they loved to talk or never said a thing. There was one dude who made it back, never said a thing, and six months later his brains were found next to a whiskey bottle. I said one dude, one dude that I knew, but there were several. Dan was that dude never wanting to talk about it and something that worried me.

I wanted Dan to like me replaying every movement, sometimes kind and sometimes not, fatherly and fair. When unkind it was to teach me a lesson. Often making a physical gesture, such as grabbing my shoulder or giving me a half hug to say, 'I got you son'. Words and gestures a father would say of encouragement and advice. I wanted to hear more, advice on life, advice on love.

My respect for Dan grew daily, now more than admiration. A new level of feeling developed, being around him comforted me. I want to be close to him, my mind saying, 'stay he'll protect you'. How could I not think that? The small farm was perfect, Dan working tirelessly to make it that way.

That's where it started but the emotional trap was set before I even knew. Long before wanting Jessie to give me a darn good blow job, long ago coming from a decrepit family with no guidance. How could Ma take me aside and tell me what to do? That was Pa's job and he never did it. Now my youthful mind took another path.

It was up to me to keep up with Dan, do as much as he, otherwise I'd disappoint him, especially now while struggling with a sick wife. I never wanted to let him down, period. After fourteen hours strength lingered, merely pushing cow shit. Early darkness hadn't brought out the screeching creatures who dominate night noise. My heart pumped at the thought of seeing Dan, wanting to tell him about all my achievements.

A brilliant smile appeared on my face when the sound broke, an engine. I was anxious to see them, finishing my jobs half-heartedly, racing back, bursting through the door.

Dan eyed me suspiciously. "Everything all right son."

"Oh, fine…everything is fine." My expression gave everything away. In his company I didn't think about home as his lips broadened, cheeks rising offering a broad-appealing smile.

I had to ask. "How's Martha?

"Don't know, not doing so well."

It hurt him to say it. I wanted to pry deeper into their business, boyish curiosity taking over, resisting at the last-minute, biting my lip before deciding to please him, stating. "Did everything you said," standing to attention waiting for approval, but none came.

All he said was, "Good, let's eat," going to the kitchen.

We found ham and composed a meal accompanied with eggs, peas from the garden, and peaches. Those to ripe to be sent to market, only four.

"Well," Dan said after a deathly silence. "Seems like it will be just us boys for a few days."

"We'll survive," trying to be stoical, exchanging smiles.

Dan lifted his hand placing it on my shoulder, fingers gripping worn muscle.

"You did a good job today. Thanks! That's a lot of bushels."

Hearing him say it made my heart race, approval from my real Pa never came. The warm feeling started in my stomach, radiated through my body repairing damaged parts of my soul. His hand moved to the base of my neck, squeezing harder, liking the touch, the small massage feeling good. His eyes simultaneously sad and happy.

My throat suddenly dry, whispered. "Thanks."

Dan volunteered. "Martha's in hospital. In a few days I'll see how she is."

"I'm very sorry," was all I could muster but Dan sensed compassion.

"You're a good boy. I can see that, right now don't know what I'd do without you."

His lips puckered, eyes welled, as if he needed comfort and I wanted to give it to him. The sun had long disappeared, nightfall upon us, crickets cried a chorus, their shrill the only real noise.

Dan got up stretching, yawning, going to his chair. "You see the paper?"

"It's right here"

I had dumped it in the kitchen, not next to his chair.

Dan moaned, "My God it's hot."

It would insult him if I strolled, rushing into the kitchen, paper not where I thought, Dan's grunts distracting. It wasn't more than two minutes, two minutes too long.

Dan sat in his broad-backed chair, whiskey in hand, stripped to his shorts and undershirt, legs slightly apart. He stopped scratching as I pulled off the sleeve, delivering it in a subservient manner. I was happy, *very happy* do that for him.

"I need a shower," before saying what I wanted to. "Can I come down and read my book afterwards?" My voice cracked with hesitation, tone low, expecting rejection.

"Cause ya can." Dan quick to respond.

I washed some of the pain away letting water hit my skin with all the force the small, shower head could muster. Not wanting excessive clothing made the same decision as Dan, putting on fresh underwear and a tee, going downstairs.

I left my book upstairs. It was heavy, out of my league and wasn't sure what discussion it would bring. Dan's chair was in front of a bureau, next to a gun case, in the middle old newspapers collected. He barely noticed me selecting one, mind buried in the days' news.

I couldn't look at him, not directly, trying to select an article. Out the corner of my eye Dan sipped while his other hand scratched, the man being himself. If I had an itchy ball problem, I'd be scratching. There is no reason to think about it, except I didn't have any male role models in my early youth. The usual bonding a maturing male brain needs never occurring, liking the simplicity of male interaction. He didn't care, I didn't care.

I read some articles, had to, not being able to fake read for than a minute or two. The front page was dominated with State news, but it wasn't long before the pages descended to Jackson High's achievements, an appeal for help after someone's home burned, a few advertisements and in the legal section an article about a land dispute. I only read it because there was a mention of Benton. Alright v Brown. Some old bod divided up his land on word, heirs on good terms at the time. That had changed apparently with someone claiming 8 acres.

Dan's hands moved in a sequence, turn the page, take a sip, scratch or adjust his junk which was never happy. He got up, arching his back, pushing his pelvis forward, fly buttons undone, blond hair exposed. I've lost count the number of times he caught me looking.

"I'm out of here. Good night, switch everything off."

It wasn't long before I followed. Dan in his bedroom, door ajar, trying to create a breeze, lay on his side, one leg over the other, white cotton stretching over his glutes. I was happy he could find peace, at a time like this, wanting to share that, share his every thought, standing in the doorway hearing him breathe, the sound calming, not wanting to move, listening for several minutes.

I liked the image, my hands caressing tension and pain from his body as he repeated, 'Good job son' and 'Thanks son', teasing away his and my sorrow one muscle at a time.

I wanted to lay next to him taking one step forward, something stopping me. I winced when turning to my room, remembering leaving feeling like only survivor after a nuclear bomb, totally alone.

***

Dan scurried in the hallway, in the bathroom, toilet flushing and water splashing. It stopped, Dan standing at my doorway, towel wrapped around his waist.

"Hope you're feeling fit. Got strong man's work to do," smiling, slightly teasing. "First get your morning jobs done."

What did he mean, strong man's work? Almost every muscle ached, body insufficiently rested and numb.

Dan carried a chainsaw, an ax, ropes, and handsaws placing them in the back of a tractor.

"I'm waiting on ya."

I decided not to hurry. This man had endless energy, however, the milk had to be at the bottom of the lane soon. I was pushing the cart like the only Egyptian carrying a sphinx when the truck came barreling down the road. I didn't want to be late, pushing harder, milk churns vibrating towards the edge. The lane was not perfect with a large flat stone and a drop. I knew but forgot, the cart fell toppling a churn, force pushing off the lid and a white wave flowed. The other teetered on the edge of a similar fate which I grabbed with both hands, abandoning the cart scampering the remaining thirty feet to meet a viscous driver.

"By God, you need a whooping."

I turned to the mess, heart sinking. Not knowing what to tell Dan picking up the empty churn, pulling the cart, head held low, engrossed in the various scenarios of how Dan would react. Would he simply take the money out of my pay, make me drink water as my father would have done, along with a thrashing of course, or would he simply yell and scream?

I did not see him, only his shadow at first, standing at the top of the lane, fists on his hips, laughing hard, bend over, having trouble catching his breath.

"Oh, that was funny. What is up with you son?"

"I'm sorry," trying to stare him in the eye to show sincerity, which was impossible as Dan still laughing.

"That's the funniest darn thing I've seen in years," he exclaimed, uncertain if his reaction was making me feel better, because he wasn't apoplectic, or worse …foolish. Except I was foolish, and his reaction was honest. Dan was human, laughing off my error deepened my faith in him. It was over, no need to clarify the mistake.

"I'm really sorry," whimpering. "It's… I'm tired from yesterday."

"Tired," Dan cried. "If you're tired now wait until the end of today."

My words angered him, tone and facial expressions changing from humor to anger, eyebrows raised, jaw clenched, chin bunched up. All from my naive comment.

"Get moving." Dan shouted like a sergeant to a recruit, striding to the tractor. He took off the handbrake, cranked the ignition and hit the gas. He made me take extra footage, sprinting, throwing myself in the trailer. Dan grinned- why was he testing me?

The cumbersome machine halted near the spot I marked shortly after my arrival, and admittedly several times since. We selected trees to be felled, Dan bringing them down before I took over, segmenting limbs from trunks. This is winter firewood. We labored in the heat, my mind ignoring the pain. I couldn't complain anyway.

There was little exchange except orders which didn't always come in a pleasant manner. Dan's mannerisms made the atmosphere animalistic especially when the trees refused to compromise with his wishes. He expected me to be the same. I wanted to do the same, it solves the pain issue.

Sweat poured, needing more hydration, hoping Dan would take a second quick break, time ticked, there was none. The sun had long passed its pinnacle, endless labor creating muscles spasms and cramps, Dan chuckling. The evidence of our labor accumulated.

Finally, Dan broke the silence. "Last one son."

I was relieved, treating the last tree with anger before collapsing in a sulky slump.

"I'm hungry and thirsty." Dan exclaimed, as if I wasn't. "You want too cool off?"

"Whatever," I said in a spiteful manner.

I heard him sigh. "Tilt your head back boy." In no time he was pouring remaining canteen water on my face, opening my mouth to catch whatever I could.

"Feel better?"

I guess the answer is yes, but I would have preferred to have done it myself.

Dan took a small sack out the tractor and marched. We followed the stream, Dan was all business while we worked, his jovial demeanor returning.

"Common son, you worked hard. Don't you want to have some fun?"

The trees diminished before a verge on one side of Dan's pond, as he called it. I knew it wasn't exactly his pond brushing off the mis-representation. It was a tranquil place, trees and bushes collecting on the other side creating an overhang wondering if the pond was stocked and with what types of fish?

Dan lay, taking deep breaths, enjoying the air. "Come on eat," smile benevolent, the same as day one. In the hessian sack were peaches, bread and spam. I was angry and wanted him to pay, in some form, perhaps information.

"You never had kids?"

Dan smirked. "Well son, no," pausing, editing himself. "We tried, married since twenty-two. Guess it wasn't meant to be."

Not giving up. "Did you want to have kids?"

Dan took a deep breath straightening hunched shoulders, chin leveling, eyes demanding I stare into them.

"I would have dearly liked kids, a son, daughter, maybe more," his eyes misting, fantasizing about younglings running around the pond, 'Daddy watch me', before jumping in making the biggest splash. Dan would rise to his feet in applause, yet his proud smile was never meant to be.

His feeling of regret moved in like a storm. Dan experiencing more, a sense of loss, a space he was never allowed to enter and one he so desperately wanted to occupy. I wanted to recognize that, my hand stretching out, placing it firmly above his knee. I kept steady eye contact, increasing my grip to clearly signify support. He twisted his neck in an effort to shake off pain, physical and mental. Dan was down but not out.

"I'm cooling off," standing up, "Come on, it's time for a swim."

Dan unbuckled his pants kicking off his shoes. Surprised, staring at him, socks were off, pants and underwear down in one go.

I was hot, muscles burned, nothing sounded better than the thought of cool water. Body hair soaked in sweat made my clothes stick, wanting the liberating feeling of ripping them off. Dan waited for me to strip giving my junk a three-second look. Since he was looking at me, I looked at him, swollen testicles, penis not exactly looking at the ground.

Dan's body sprang into the air. Muscled buttocks formed the top of a flying arc as he dove into the water, body making minimal splash, reappearing in the middle.

"Come on," Dan shouted paddling backward, splashing his feet, wanting to observe my dive. I wasn't going to disappoint, despite my bulk there were minimal waves, swimming underwater coming up to Dan splashing me in the face. Energized and ready for horseplay thought he was a buddy, dunking him deep.

Dan arose challenging, "Oh, you want to play." He grabbed my head pushing down, my face racing towards his groin as he tried to leapfrog over me. His athletics were good, but not that good, testicles hitting my forehead, penis brushing over my hair. It didn't matter we were having fun! Isn't naked horseplay a part of male bonding? I wish I had a brother, wish my uncles hadn't fallen in Vietnam and wish I had a real father. None of this would be necessary otherwise.

We cavorted, playing as hard as we could, racing from end to end, swimming underwater for as long as possible, attacking each other with water sprays whenever we got the chance. Exhilarated, after hours of tension, we flopped onto the bank, bodies facing the sun, inhaling, exhaling.

Dan still gasping, "You thirsty son?"

"Thinking about sippin' some out of the pond," Breaking into unnecessary laughter.

"Be right back." Dan's smile was endearing. I wanted him to like me, now I think he does. I worked hard, played hard and earned respect.

Dan's physique showed how a mature man could retain his body. Perfectly placed muscles weren't created from vanity but out of necessity, hard work carved this sculpture. He disappeared into the depths leaving me to wonder what's going on! Seconds passed, each seeming longer than the other, finally, his body broke the surface like a God, glee on his face, each hand held high filled with a golden trophy.

Stumbling back Dan giggled like a boy seeing girl's knickers for the first time, "Always keep a crate down there. That way ya know they're gonna be cool."

I looked at the label, 'Schaefer Beer'. Except for a few stolen sips I'd never drank. Having the bottle in my hand made me feel like a man. It was mine and able to drink and enjoy without criticism, judgment free.

My first sip was small, Dan chugged. I took larger gulps to quench my first and to compete. The flavor was slightly bitter yet smooth, mellow and pleasing, needing more. Both bottles were empty, discarded on the grass, signs of our desperate need for refreshment. Dan pointed to where the beer crate lay. Unchallenged, I returned equally triumphant handing over one of the glistening bottles. Dan swiped my outer thigh, a friendly gesture to confirm work well done.

This time we savored the liquid, lying back gazing at the sky.

Several minutes went by, alcohol entering my brain, faintly hearing Dan asking, "You got a girlfriend?"

Oh Jessie! The women plagued me and didn't want to think about her, especially now, but I had to answer. "Yeah."

He interpreted the single word. "Well, you don't seem very happy about it."

"Oh, kinda of, well, I don't know…complicated." The message garbled from alcohol soaking deeper into brain tissue, unchecked words and feelings sprang to mind and body. You start out slow, that is what alcohol does, small admissions at first but eventually, not necessarily today, but one day, guts spill, emotional raw guts.

"She's very pretty, Jessie… nice," making a gesture indicating her breasts were large. Like a juvenile I sniggered, Dan following suit as if neither of us had ever seen a pair. My snigger was innocent, his wasn't.

"You've had her a few times then?" Dan interjecting, voice deep, fatherly, monotone.

This was a tricky question to answer. The alcohol made me giddy and uninhibited, wanting to say, 'Yeah, fuck her all the time,' except that wasn't true.

Addled I tried to double-check my words. "When we met, she was all over me, but it was only the once and was it good. Since then she's been, well kinda quiet. Like she doesn't want it."

No one could have expected Dan's response, roaring with laughter. He laughed at me earlier in the day when I split the milk, that was acceptable. My foolishness deserved mockery. Now it was something else, naivety, stupidity. I don't know what, just harder to take.

I tried to justify the statement blurting, "She's done it with her hands a few times."

A line that didn't make things better, serving as more amusement to his mature mind.

He rolled on his side, looked directly at me, the full elegance and expanse of his body accentuated by sunlight, held out a finger and pointed. "Now listen boy," letting out an unapologetic burp. "They always do that."

"What?" It was clear from my duped face he needs to explain.

"Well, girls like to give a taste, then it's very little or nothing until a ring is on," pointing at that finger, rolling back, bathing in the sanctity of knowledge.

"Really," feeling cheated, a sucker, just another male for the firing line.

"Oh, yeah son, Martha was no different. When we first met, all she wanted to do was kiss. I was real shy at the time and one night she opened her bra. They were right in front of my face, still I wouldn't touch them. She took my hands and made me ..." My eyes wide open. "…before moving my hand down between her legs."

Dan pointing at his own groin accentuating the point, his cock moving on his belly.

If another man points to his groin as part of a conversation that does not mean you look, never able to keep a single element of bro code in Dan's presence.

Dan deflected the faux pas, continuing, "I was young, scared, but then she takes down my pants and sticks my cock into her and rode me like a cowgirl."

This sounded comparable to my experiences with Jessie, definitely in the same vein, being one fuck and three hand jobs into the relationship.

Dan concluded. "Spent almost two years trying to get her to do that again. It was the night of our wedding…not the same," looking regretful, despondent, a person in need of consolation.

55

I wanted to look at him and not at 'him', but Dan moved closer. Initially he scratched like he always did before turning to gingerly flicks, blood flow an irritation, swelling, quivering.

The sun, the alcohol, the testosterone, the talk of sex made my body react in ways unimaginable, every inch tingling. It was the speed that took me, not needing to look knowing my own was soaking up blood.

I wasn't going to be able to control it, not if I lay here. I couldn't run into the bushes or into the pond as that would make Dan laugh. But I wasn't alone, Dan now fully erect, head deep-red, bulbous, veins meandering up his shaft like deep blue rivers. He lay silently, bathing in the sun, an intense yearning escalating, signals bouncing between our bodies, heart rate increasing.

Dan, rolled back onto his side, making sure he had my attention. "You know what." Voice lowered, "Sometimes we don't need 'em."

His hand went down to his crotch, stroking, tossing his balls around, softly and naturally. Dan's eyes left mine to fix them on my erection. I stared at his.

There was silence, yet a loud sound thumped in my head like a warrior's drumbeat, my throat parched despite refreshment. Normally I rubbed my thigh, then touched myself as naturally as possible, taking a few swipes and flicking my balls the same way he did. Dan responded doing the same again, our eyes dancing between face and crotch.

Dan mixed it up, hand wrapping his shaft taking long strokes from the base to the tip. When reaching the top, he took in a deep breath, before sliding downwards letting out a sigh of satisfaction.

I didn't know what to think, apart from knowing I wanted this to happen, but didn't know what 'this' was. He was masturbating, and I wanted to do that. Was I going to touch him? Was he going to touch me?

For my first time I would have preferred a simple jack off session. Most dudes do that much younger to get it out of their system. I guess another part of male bonding, but none of that happened in the puritanical society of my youth. I felt guilty, most do, but moved my hand anyway, eyes no longer locked, our vision focused on each other masturbating.

I kidded myself that none of this was intended and whatever was happening naturally materialized. Of course, Dan knew exactly what was going to happen.

"Feels good?" Dan's voice deep, created from satisfaction, tones originating deep in his gut.

"Yeah," as quietly as I could.

Perhaps it was the small nod when I said 'Yeah' that gave him the go ahead. He took his hand of his cock and rested it on my thigh, smoothing out his palm following the contours of my quadriceps, touch rough, brittle working man skin.

Dan was touching me. My question answered. His hand explored my body sliding to my buttocks. His hands were large, my butt muscle larger, grabbing beef and massaging it before tracing my crack, brushing my balls.

I forgot everything I was ever told about touching other men. I knew it was bullshit, the desire bursting through my body proved it was. Dan sensed it, his body increasingly closer, faces within inches, nothing but a small canyon between us. His feet touched mine, hand massaged my hip, my inner thigh then he touched it. I didn't say stop when crossing the last barrier, liking being fondled. Always wanting someone to touch me.

His hand moved to my belly, ruffling my fur and bush, then went back and started at the base, touching me this time with purpose like I expected a man to.

I fully realized what I was doing, this was happening. It wasn't me wanting to stand next to another boy, nor the vendor, it was me enjoying myself with another man. After thinking about it for so long it's unbelievable at first, like the moment I inserted myself into Jessie. A whole lot of growing up happened in a short while. Dan sensed what I was thinking.

"It's okay we're just a pair of guys helping each other out."

"Yeah."

Dan thought I wasn't convinced.

"It's better than doing it alone, sure as hell no ladies around who are gonna do it for us. Not without wanting something back."

We chuckled about the pragmatic attitude to sex.

"Yeah, got that one right." Trying to be off the cuff.

Dan was always acutely aware of another's emotions. I'd thought about this for so long and liked it more than ever dreamed. I liked it because I liked Dan. He was right, it wasn't weird or wrong. My eyes must have softened. He knew I was ready.

Dan came even closer and instinctively I backed off, yet he moved like a predator, a large cat moving in, pushing me with clear force. I lay flat on the grass, his hands touched my body, one on my thigh and another on my pectorals pinching my nipples. My eyelids sank, without vision his touch only grew in intensity. He massaged my testicles while rubbing my belly, felt his hand on my cock, stroking gently, every nerve sending shock waves. Then he crossed another barrier.

I felt something soft swipe across my cockhead and again in my pee hole. I had to look, lips were parted, tongue lashing out like a snake, darting in and out, licking. His mouth opened, my cock disappearing and couldn't believe it. He closed his lips, a warm silky sensation growing as his mouth enveloped every inch. His face embedded in my groin, my dark bush like weeds sprouting from his mouth, holding my cock deep in his throat, face growing red in a self-imposed oral grip only to repeat the action; hovering on the top, tongue like a hummingbird looking for nectar before devouring my meat. My cock was fatter than his mouth, but he didn't struggle. He liked burying it, sticking out his tongue and licking my balls, leaving sticky saliva on my hairy sack. He kept going back trying to stick his tongue into my meatus like a game, squeezing then admiring the mini liquid crystal balls before swiping them away with the tip of this tongue.

He made his mouth a pussy, all the time massaging my balls, my inner thigh. His fingertips travelled south, coming closer pulling the hair around it, so close but not there, circling the circumference, tapping the soft spot in the middle. I liked this, but only this, don't go deeper, taking deep breaths.

I wanted long strokes taking control of his head guiding my dick in and out of his mouth, Dan looking up in surprise beginning to work a little harder. It was too much, lips, fingers, tongue and throat teasing every nerve-ending spurred the beginning.

The feeling began in my prostate, much deeper than ever before, my sexuality like a series of caves and now I was exploring another cavern. My scrotum contracted, balls inside my body, skin on my shaft stretching, glans about to burst with blood no place to go. Dan knew what was happening and knew what to do, wrapping his thumb and forefinger under my head, getting the first sense of how long this orgasm was going to last. Semen escalated, brain releasing huge amounts of endorphins, holding onto my ecstasy.

Dan's grip tricked my junk into thinking it hasn't done its job, pumping more semen, my penis pulsated. All laws of physics broken small spurts splashed onto his lips, his head moved slightly, a gush hit his cheeks and a third on his forehead. Dan accepted the rest on his face, nose and chin. Down from an extraordinary high Dan looked up, cum slithering over his lips, smiling and giggling. I did the same.

He wiped his face, sat up, supporting himself with an elbow, penis standing straight out. He looked at it, then back at me.

This is a difficult situation. Not because I was nineteen and had no idea what I was doing, but playing with another dude after I've blown my wad is usually out of the question. There are few exceptions, just how it is, my interest in dick disappearing like the white dove at the end of a magician's show. Of course, the bird is never actually dead, due to reappear in about a month. In this case there was no point in thinking about it, not knowing anything and I tried.

"Okay!" In the same playful, challenging voice we used while messing around in the pond, pushing him back, moving quickly so couldn't second-guess myself, wrapping my hand around, masturbating him hard and fast.

"Hey slow down son. It's supposed to feel real nice."

I got what he was saying, my hand aggressive, awkward, pretending it's my own cock, spitting on my hand continuing with long, slow lubricated stokes.

Dan let out a small moan and said, "That's a start boy."

He was enjoying it, but I wanted to give him more satisfaction caressing his tightening hairy sack. Dan looked up to check progress, nodding towards his cock. Oh, he wanted more, spitting, using longer strokes from the base to the very tip, twisting my fist at the final moment for extra pleasure. Dan moaned but still looking up intermittently, raising his pelvis. I tickled his pee hole while tickling his balls. It feels good when that piece of skin between balls and ass is massaged trying that, Dan squirming from the pleasure raising his pelvis again, finger resting on his butt hole. I liked that a lot as well, why wouldn't Dan, pressing lightly against his anus, sweaty and soft, my fingertip circling. I was concentrating and didn't hear Dan's moan and grunts getting louder. His cock couldn't get harder and scrotum contracted. I moved my hand from his hole grabbing his balls tightly while working his shaft faster.

"Oh, God!" Dan's lungs heaved. "Johnnie please…sssuu…"

I caressed my thumb and forefinger around the head, my other working the remainder of his shaft. I wanted to make it last, for him.

Dan's eyes remained a pendulum between his cock and my mouth, gasped and then pushed my head towards it.

I wanted to try putting his cock in my mouth but was getting used to having another man in my hand. I liked the feeling mostly how turgid it was, the muscle, the big vein and all the little veins supporting an organ normally flaccid. Normally just a pee let out. Now it's something different, no longer a dick but a cock. Genitalia have a distinctive smell.

I wasn't ready for it in my mouth, starting with caressing my lips over the tip getting first ideas of the taste. He wanted more pushing my head down, my teeth hitting soft tissue.

"Fuck boy!" Dan wincing, a red strip appearing. His face filled with urgency.

"Sorry."

60

He gripped me by the neck and said, "Suck it". More of a command than a request.

It was more puckering than opening my mouth, Dan's shaft barely a quarter of the way in, cock head massaging my tongue. I wanted to also use my hands trying to bring greater satisfaction and didn't understand him tugging them away.

The bit that bothered me was when his palm hit the back of my head. Yes, I did the same thing to him but now I had no control. Let me go deeper, slowly in my own time, brushing his hand off when he wanted to push me. I can do this, thinking I want to do it, shutting my eyes, lips opening feeling the contours of his shaft before it hit my tonsils and backed off. I tried again.

Dan groaned. "Please boy."

I thought I was edging him, thought he liked it and needed air taking his cock out of my mouth.

"Boy, no boy, don't stop now."

It was too late, his body completely rigid, every muscle tense, toes stretched out. Dan started his orgasm, a pungent fluid appearing at the surface, fishy and eggy. Dan growled letting out his first full stream too heavy to make into the air, fingers digging into the grass continuing to ejaculate. His semen, some tinged yellow, some white, both thick and clear mottled on his belly and chest is a memory that stays. When I see the effect in works of art always think of those few seconds while I studied his life, wondering if the artist has the same thought.

Dan's breathing slowed, taking my hand away, eyes opened. He stared at me. We didn't giggle.

"Looks like we need another swim," Dan's eyebrows bunched.

I tried to talk to him on the way back, asking him if there were fish in the pond and what types. He grunted and I never brought up the subject again.

***

I made work routine, recent events playing in my mind, not minding, wanting to see this movie time and time again. I like what happened wishing I had more time.

61

Dan opened a can of beans slicing spam before a bad attempt at eggs. He seemed irritated with the pan tossing the food on the plate. We said nothing throughout dinner.

Dan was suddenly a different person from earlier, the life, boyhood nature displayed by the pond replaced with anger and frustration of a child trying to hit a Piñata and always missing. As he stumbled into the living room the realization that I'd forgotten his paper was chilling.

Seconds later thunder blasted through the walls. "Where's my paper?"

The day was long, and I hadn't had time is what I thought.

Poised next to his chair, aggression mounting. "Go get me my paper."

"Sorry been busy up to now," said in a way that could not offend anyone. Dan's sight almost led me out the door.

Getting to the box was no worry, more was the example of Dan's fluctuating mood. Surprised at the unnecessary acrimony I hesitated before giving him the paper.

"Thank you," he said spitefully, ripping it open, eyeing me with a tight face. "Good night."

It was difficult to sleep, eventually putting Dan's changing frame of mind down to Martha being in hospital. While doing my daily mental housekeeping it was a good place to explain Dan's volatility at the time, even though not entirely accurate.

It wasn't my imagination running wild, instead, what he did this afternoon showed experience. I couldn't stand the thought of Dan with another man. More so, the possible temporary nature of our relationship, that I'd come and go like a pesky problem, hating the feeling of being insignificant. My soul was shattered wanting to be a part of someone's life.

Who were these other guys? I knew the answer; boi 1973, boi 1972. I was boi 1974. My heart tried to escape not wanting to accept any form of reality. My face reddened quietly seething, mind bursting with scenes of bloody vengeance only a full flood of jealousy brings, sleeping maybe ninety minutes that night, and not many hours over the next few days.

***

"Hey, buddy got something for ya.... wanna help out?" He was trying to cook breakfast. "You're a better cook anyhow."

The other Dan was back. We were simply two good friends trying to get through a bad situation. That changed after mid-morning, every move followed by peeling eyes. When I made mistakes, he chuckled at some and sneered at others.

Dinner meant sitting face to face. He ate without conviction setting his fork on the plate, a burp the only sign of satisfaction. When his eyes twinkled good Dan was home.

"What wrong with Martha?" I inquired.

"Heart."

"Oh!" surprised, "but that doesn't mean she going to…" Dan broke me off.

"Doc said it's all diseased."

I didn't understand except knew from Ma's book it was serious, realizing my question was morbid and stupid feeling embarrassed excused myself and cleared the table.

My foot was on the first step towards my room.

"Hey, son!"

It's not what he said but the tone. Those two words can come out in a thousand forms, from the love of father to the warning of you're about to kill yourself.

"Yeah!"

"Ya, doing a good job son. Real good."

I turned, he finished his first tumbler, the initial hit of alcohol relaxing him, there was no smell of soap, crotch of his shorts blotched yellow.

His chair was large, upholstered, ideally wanting to sit on his lap and for him to tell me stories that were interesting and taught life lessons. Our eyes locked, Dan stretched, took off his undershirt, a forefinger caressed his left nipple, a hand meandered downwards. It wasn't a decision it was a reaction, going to bed without using the bathroom. I did it because my body was intoxicated with hormones, every fucking hormone.

I'd seen two Dan's, admittedly 'this' guy was amiable, but I knew he could take me to places where I wasn't ready to go. I wanted to play, wad ready, simply knew he'll dominate me. What happens when the day comes he wants what I don't want? He'd make a play for it, he's human and very much a man. Getting fucked up the ass is like having a reverse constipated poop over and over again. I don't want that and why I ran, him expecting it, imagining the other boys giving it to him. The cocktail of emotion, from intrigue to disgust back to jealousy, was worse than drinking bad moonshine.

What I wanted is for Dan to take me in his arms, cuddle me, kiss me on the lips, ear, and throat telling me everything is fine, time and time again. We'd grind, mixing it up with mouth for the taste and feeling rather a desire to get face-fucked.

This is not what I should be thinking about, however, and maybe also why I ran having a big problem at the back of my head for days, ever since I got the letter. My mind should concentrate on writing an apology to Jessie needing; paper, envelope and a stamp, starting a mental draft.

'We have known each other for two years and I have always shown respect. What happened was not like me, I am sorry.'

Woefully insufficient. A dozen sonnets with endless amorous whispers would not work either. Only one thing would, that statement: "I love you." The single way out of trouble was to write it down which I didn't want to do. All nineteen-year olds in their right minds don't want to do that even though our dicks make us say it frequently when seeing pussy but there was no pussy. The one time I did say was for a hot mouth, which I didn't get if anyone recalls.

***

Dan had been pleasant, mostly. It was Saturday night, offering me a beer.

"Hey, gotta do something bad before going to the Lord and sayin' sorry," he joked.

My thoughts hadn't strayed much for days, the letter, Dan, the letter. It was difficult to re-engage with him, but in many ways harder not to, as he noticed my distance began repeating his standard compliment. "You're doing a good job son."

If anyone doesn't get this, statements like, 'Please to have you around', 'Good job son' and even 'Good boy', feel good. These sentences new to my hearing, made me melt like ice cream after hot chocolate sauce is poured on top.

We talked on and off, my nervousness apparent.

"What's up son."

I was going to tell him about Jessie but instead. "It's been hard so far," suppressing tears sourced from exhaustion.

Dan stood back opening his arms. "Hey buddy boy you're right, things have been a little tough around here, lately."

It's not in my nature to dwell. Life was frequently to confusing anyway, like being given a math problem you were never meant to solve. I looked down and away giving me time to consider, my thought interjected.

"You know how to play poker?"

"No," as if denying a felony.

"Great, let's have some fun. It's Saturday night and I'll teach you poker." Dan sounded completely convinced this was a great idea, standing up, arms high, stretching.

I simply said, "Yes," because I couldn't say 'No'.

"Common boy I am going to get a smile out of you," getting cards, starting to shuffle.

I had no experience playing hands, but knew it was about working odds from watching my uncles play. That was a long time ago. Dan explained the game before we played but won none of the first three hands. He eyed me, I eyed him back.

He was going to know I will forgive him, but there was going to be a price. At first, he laughed it off as beginner's luck, but my stare remained as he folded another hand, slowly realizing I was serious and how serious I could be. I let my mood relax, confidence growing with the predominant amount of chips flowing my way. Being in control warmed my body.

Dan didn't like it. "I don't want you to be the smart one."

Unintentionally Dan revealed a piece of himself, quick to realize the mistake, deciding to reach for more hard liquor. He offered a shot to celebrate my victory which I took graciously, wanting to push the conversation forward trying to pluck enough courage to ask for a stamp, envelope, and paper. Dan realized I was disingenuous shutting down any late-night chatter.

"I want to be early for church, haven't been in a while. Everyone's asking about Martha." Dan stood, instantaneously doing the same thing.

He was right in front of me and I would have to move to let him by. I didn't know what I wanted at that point as he killed the conversation. I couldn't even say he was a bad looser as he offered me a drink. I just wanted to be emotionally closer.

"What's wrong John?"

John, my respect name.

I should have said need to write a letter but for some weird reason said. "Sometimes you're really friendly and sometimes you're not."

"Common son, I don't want to be like that," Dan hesitating, "You know we have to work together."

Dan moved forward, opening his big frame, not overly close. We weren't touching apart from his arm over my shoulder and a chest bump, a semi-embrace, our faces close. A basic instinct, my hand went to his waist, his breath pounded my skin, a desert wind.

"Thank you, John." Pulling me closer, our bodies touched, the pressure increasing holding the hug for several seconds. For those seconds I didn't have a care in world forgetting Jessie, my tortured upbringing, everything.

"I think you'd better go to bed." His voice soft and commanding but I didn't want this to stop. Don't you understand, if you hug me I can forget?

***

One thing changed at church. Simon had stopped looking at me the whole time, as since last week, we decided to sit next to each other. Dan frowned but we were good, most of the time, me passing only one note.

It was amusing the Sherriff was never in church but was always there immediately afterward, to see if there was any food. Today was no exception rolling up as the crowd left the chapel. There was something different about him today, smiling when he looked at me, keeping the same expression as I walked past observing my every move, sight mostly at waist level. It was the first inkling the Sherriff is a complex person.

***

I meandered to the pond, wasn't hot, earth not shimmering, sky dotted with wistful cotton-ball clouds and a soft wind keeping temperatures down. It didn't matter, always hating my clothes, removing my shirt. As the breeze swelled the sun caught a thousand ripples, a flash of light bouncing off the pond. I flopped on the verge lazily kicking off my shoes pushing down my pants, flicking them aside with my foot.

Being naked was being free, every piece of clothing I wore day in and out nothing more than a shackle. Clothes are restraining and defining, characteristics that don't mix well with human nature. Wearing doctor's clothes doesn't make me able to cure, expensive clothes don't mean I'm rich, and soiled clothes don't make me dirty.

What should I do about Jessie? She plagued my mind like a cancer. The resistance was not wanting to say, 'I love you', being a flat lie. A flat lie is like a very small flat earth. You will fall off.

However, if I did say 'it', the chances of Jessie telling her bodyguards brothers were high. Especially if wrote a sonnet to put Shakespeare to shame, scented the envelope placing tear drops and rose petals inside. I'm far from that guy, even if I really did love her. My mother bought the biology book to use my fascination with nature in the hope of improving my reading and writing abilities. It mostly worked, but I've never written a letter and certainly never written what I'm supposed to feel on paper. Would have been a whole lot easier if I felt something, that I knew. In the interim, I'd have to apologize, explain, lie, write down anything to get her out of my head, trying for the umpteenth time to compose and failing after the first sentence.

67

I swam frenzied in every direction, my hands not cupped, fists slamming the surface. I swam to the bottom of the pond and stayed there enjoying the silence. This is my favorite water game. Someone said it later, 'Oh he's playing Manatee again.' Slowly I circled noticing the beer crate was empty. Who drank the remaining bottles?

I lazed in the sun, soul hovering over my body in a pleasant dreamy state. Finally my mind was blank, if only I had ten more minutes, but I sent the note that it's cool to hang, not wanting anyone to hear us making arrangements and still feeling bad about our first encounter.

"Hi John."

"Hey what's up?" Sitting up, making an effort to be sociable.

I said sorry after church today. Little tear drops accumulated in the corner of his eyes, holding it back, like I was the first person ever to say sorry. I didn't make a big deal out it, even going along with the gentle make-up handshake. In my world, we make up by grabbing each other's hand while looking each other in the eye. Exactly how firm indicates our sincerity. Simon stripped.

"Why you wear those funny shorts…" wanting a better word, "Underpants?"

"It's what we all were."

"I don't." Trying to be clever.

"You're not a Mennonite and we call them garments or simply G's. Simon, should become a teacher.

I knew something about them lot, screwing up my face, but initially too proud to ask, my curiosity unfolding. "So, what do you…?"

Simon was a polite guy realizing I couldn't formulate my question and I wasn't sure if I had a specific one anyway.

"Believe in? Same as you, the Holy Trinity." Pointing his head to the sky.

"I didn't mean that. What I believe in…is…ain't a lot" Looking at the ground sheepishly.

"Oh!" He said. I must be the first non-believer he met; Simon shocked.

"I don't get it. Why you hangin' with this lot?" I asked.

"They are Baptist, so I am sort of, and they have work. Too many mouths to feed at home."

"…get thrown out for the summer?" I joked. Sadly, it was true.

"You do if the farm is small and have eight siblings?"

One less mouth to feed. That I could relate to. "The dollars you earn go back to your family?"

Simon wasn't offended at the question but didn't answer. I was the one that looked stupid, mulling on what I'd learned. Simon wasn't an adversary, after our altercation he was friendly, sincere and that's why I made up to him. He seemed as confused and scared about life as I.

"Hey, you ever seen that bull hanging with Dan after church?"

Yeah, Simon seemed tired.

"He scares me and kinda weird, looking at me mighty funny today."

Simon almost asleep.

What a Silly Thing to Do

It was another evening of two guys sitting around in underwear, Dan sipping while I read old newspapers. I wanted to re-read the article about the land dispute, but the paper was gone.

"I'm gonna get some rest. It's a long day at that blessed hospital," he said.

"Dan," halting him halfway up the stairs. "What's up for tomorrow?"

I knew what he needed, wanting him to command me.

"You need to find each and every perfect peach in the darn place." He chuckled and thought it was funny.

"Yes, Sir!"

"Good boy," his voice raised, said like a marching order. We laughed again and I thought he was a friend.

By the time I got upstairs Dan was fast asleep, door ajar as before. Pushing panels of oak, door creaking, he stirred, in the same position as the other night, on his side, semi-fetal, shorts tight.

I stood for many minutes wondering what to do, should I, or could I considering all events curl up with him? My mind was telling me he wanted to be left alone to rest, heart telling me that is where I wanted to be, and won't stay long.

I wasn't going to disturb him, entering the room like a thief, sitting on the mattress softly, gently laying down, happy listening to the sound of his rhythmic breathing. It was comforting, pleasant, closing my eyes, mind undisturbed, and suddenly devoid of worry.

It was some hours later before I awoke to the smell of bad breath and stale sweat, opening my eyes in initial fog, then Dan's face coming into focus, bright red.

"What the fuck are you doing?" His teeth clenched; pleasant hazelnut eye-tones replaced with dark anger.

"What the fuck are you doing in our bed?" His voice getting louder.

I hesitated, suddenly fully awake, no chance to think, Dan's hands went up to my throat, long fingers having little trouble gaining a tight grip.

Dan rarely waited for an answer. "Answer me! What the fuck are you doing? That's where Martha sleeps."

I could barely breathe. "You're choking me," barely able to utter.

"Boy, you're fucking lucky I'm not whipping you," grip tightening.

"I thought…" having trouble gaining enough air.

"You thought because I sucked your dick you could come into my bedroom."

"I'm sorry… really sorry," tears welling in my eyes. I said 'sorry' because that was the best thing to say despite hating the word. In truth didn't think about anything only wanting comfort. There was no time to explain and irrelevant since the concept of comfort, specifically mutual comfort, was foreign to Dan.

"Darn right you're sorry," lips raised. Teeth clenched like a dog about to bite.

"Could you let go… please?" Struggling in a pathetic attempt to get him off. "I can't breathe," legs pounding the bed, brain throbbed, throat being crushed.

"I don't care if you can't breathe."

I could barely hear him, feet and hands pounding harder, thrusting for release to no avail, vision fading to a dark misty night, feeling my eyeballs roll back.

Dan drew my face closer, feeling his spit, violently he said, "Do that again and I'll make your back bleed," throwing me away, skull hitting the headboard, body flopping like a rag doll.

With a searing pain I gasped for air, hands grappling around my throat trying to tease oxygen into my trachea and lungs, tears streaming down my cheeks, flying off my face.

"I didn't want to be alone… I am always alone," yelling, furious at the world, the lack of love, and of course myself.

Dan stood and stared as I continued to plea. "I'm sorry, I wasn't going *to*…," not knowing what to say, "only wanted to lie next to you then leave," blubbering, face 100% percent wet.

Dan's eyes were still dark with rage, fists clenched, thinking he was going to hit me. His silence frustrating, wishing he would say something and accept my apology, but he just stood there bunched up with the stance of a Neanderthal, hall light behind him creating the silhouette of a silver screen monster.

I pleaded again, "I thought… didn't know…sorry!" head swinging from side to side repeating the same words.

It's true I didn't know and wasn't thinking, something male nineteen year olds, even well-bred ones are prone too. Evidence is jails filled with 'lifers', guys who made crazy mistakes when kids, never remotely understanding what they were doing.

"You're still in our bed," Dan snarled.

I picked myself up, had trouble standing, throat on fire, staggering towards the door.

Dan threatened. "Stay the fuck out of our room." Slamming the door shut.

I did the same thing, in a stupid 'two can play that game' way, yelling and shouting things I no longer remember, frustrated inaudible words, plunging into my bed, sobbing.

I'd never been so humiliated, never felt so ashamed, impossible to take my face out of the pillow even to see light, never mind my surroundings and especially Dan.

What happened between us wasn't my idea and occurred because I felt free and happy, partially intoxicated from my first beer. It also happened because I liked him, felt safe with him. I wasn't going to touch him, wasn't even going to stay. He should never have known, more tears swelled. Now Dan hated me, I've lost him, forcing my hand into my mouth quelling despair.

Dan moved in his room; door opened. He wasn't heading downstairs but towards my room. A rush swept through my body leaving it cold with pure, white fear. The door opened, impossible to look at him.

"Listen, boy! I'm not going to spend all night listening to you whimpering. Either I throw you out or you shut-up." His voice calm considering the message.

I was angry, not only because I wasn't completely to blame but because he called me boy again, seething and spitting. "You tried to kill me, you fuck," springing out of bed, beating his chest making swipes at his face. Dan took me quickly under his control, muscles giving way because they wanted to, had to.

"I thought you were my friend. You've been kinder than …"

I didn't say it, but he knew what the missing word might be; father, Pa, Dad, parent, Pop, guardian, soul buddy, or bro. The list goes on.

Our bodies closed, Dan wrapping his arms around me, forcing my face into his chest, hairs tickling flushed cheeks. The embrace was warm and all what I wanted from the start, but the feeling was fleeting.

"You surprised me." Hands on my shoulders, shacking me like I was in a nod.

He should have hugged me longer, meaning I wasn't done complaining.

"Pa is always mean to me, beats me every chance. I thought you were…" Breaking off to the sound of his outrage.

"Get it, boy! Martha should be sleeping there!" Disgusted Dan pushed me back, falling on the bed, bordering animal he sneered and growled leaving the room. I pushed it too far. He was angry and now angrier.

***

I awoke in a pool of sweat, head heavy wanting to roll right over and disappear into my world, but the sun was already above the trees, Dan nowhere to be seen.

The cows, good as gold, were happy to see me, their large molten eyes indicating I was late. The mass of black and white creatures, racing back to their pasture, thankful I'd relieved their full udders is one I'd never forget. The image is significant because my time here could have been ideal. What would have been wrong being saturated in infatuation for a few months? Nothing!

Dan could have given me good advice for my future, helped me when I made mistakes and treated me like a son. I would have been the son he never had, if only for the summer of 1974. I hoped for a relationship that would repair the past but got none of it.

73

In my juvenile brain, I still had hope, wanting Dan to be proud showing my industrious nature, racing through cleaning the chicken coup, weeded the garden before collecting a bountiful harvest making it to the orchards marginally late.

I scoured the trees, fruit ripening continuously. If going to complete the challenge and impress Dan, there was a lot of work to do. I collected bushel after bushel laying each peach gently to rest. Dan warned the market would be critical if any are bruised. Good product meant top dollar; a fact Dan made clear. "I'm well known for quality," he harped.

Bushels mounted, onto the second orchard and the third. With respect I sped through until I gazed at the last tree, the one at the top of the lane, closest to the farmhouse.

This is my final conquest, a perfect tree on a bright green verge, a shade only imaginable by an artist with vivid taste. The sunlight created contrast, relaxing on the twisty trunk, observing peachy planets suspended above. I could catch this one last tree, after a short break, slithering to soft grass.

Since last night everything was marred, even my future. I tried to seek consolation remembering his touch, not only after the argument but every time. The memories made me feel warm. Dan didn't understand I was confused, all of this new to me, eyelids sliding.

It was too late to move. The pickup truck was racing up the driveway. Dan slowed the vehicle, standing to attention as if an army general approached. His face was blank looking at the peaches on the last tree, driving off. He was alone. Where was Martha?

I had to find out, running after him catching up as he entered the living room, shouting, "Where's Martha?"

Dan's expression remained blank. "Keep your voice down in this house," he gruffed, pointing to the front door. "You," menacingly, "Are not done yet, get out," vitriol spilling out his mouth corroding everything around.

I caught his eyes, dark and soulless reminding me of last night, the other day, the other week. I didn't like this Dan. Not the guy with bright, dancing, hazel eyes but one with dense un-resolved spaces. A chill ran over my skin, a fast knot developed in my stomach, fear carrying me outside and up the last tree.

Dan was in his chair, hands clasped to the armrests, a portion of the bottle gone. I wasn't going to talk to him, walking past efficiently. His eyes followed my every step, justifying my existence I muttered. "I'm going to make dinner."

Dan groaned, a long unsatisfied groan.

It wasn't much, the best I could do. He ate it. I wanted to know how Martha was, knowing he would say I should mind my own business. It wasn't the time.

Sleeping was tough. I thought about Jessie, the other farmhands and what he might have done to them. I thought, if Dan came into my room, what would he do? Downstairs he stumbled, labored, tripping trying to make it to the bathroom, then urinating directly into the little pool of water at the bottom of the toilet. Guys who are, or think they are, dominant always make the maximum bathroom noise. They sing, leave smells and peeing always has to be a loud waterfall.

"Oh shit," having apparently pissed on himself. That'll teach him. Dan thumped the walls to support his drunken body as clambered up the stairs. Bedsprings rang out into the night like an out-of-tune musical instrument.

Dan left early again, starting shortly after, searching for writing material heading to Dan's desk. He was an organized person hoping this was not going to be a problem. There were four little drawers on each side, quickly rummaging through. I spent all night wondering if he'd notice.

I avoided asking Dan directly as he'd ask questions, which if I failed in answering would want clarification, followed by conceivable contradiction- a trap that I'd fall into. This way I could simply write the letter and give it to the postman. No one here has to know I sexually assaulted my girlfriend.

All the side drawers were empty, in the bottom panel was a pad and pen. Not there without an envelope and stamp beginning a thorough inspection of his small office space.

Dan had a lot of bills, mostly from Trinity Memorial Hospital, some were reminders. Deeper in the pile were legal bills and threats to repossess the pickup and milking equipment. All were leased. Was Dan in financial trouble? Still early in the season with a lot of money in the orchards I didn't know. Certainly, Dan was not the huge success I thought. The realization you are being deceived is hard to take especially when the heart is involved. You kinda of, sort of, maybe try to ignore it.

The clock chimed creating a chill. In the next 45 minutes there were two pick-ups, fruit and milk. I opened the gate, ran to the barn moved a quarter of the bushels, ran back fixing up the top four cows, then moved more bushels. The first four let me know when they were done, swapping them for the next best four, moved more bushels, four more cows and time was up.

There was no time to milk the final four, the second churn not completely full. Two full churns had to be recorded or he'd forfeit. He didn't cry over spilt milk the first time, but considering he needed every cent, doubted he'd be so quick to forgive a second mishap, due to me, nosing around into his personal business.

I saw the hose, looked at the difference, no one would ever know. The churns were almost curbside when the driver pulled up.

"Late again?"

The driver didn't like me, but I didn't like him, probably the ugliest human alive, both tall and fat, hairy, bearded, with a broad monkey face. I smiled knowing of the forthcoming deception. He paused, taking the churn with fourteen gallons of milk and three gallons of water eyeing me suspiciously, checking the weight, lifting it up twice to be sure. He should have looked inside, would have been obvious to his eye. He knew I was up to something but didn't know what.

"You need a good whoopin' boy."

I smiled hearing the peach truck, waving. "Have a good day Sir!"

The peach driver guy was already at the top of the lane before I made it back, equally unimpressed. "I haven't got all day."

I went to the hen house, fried their eggs, feeling better with the rush of protein hitting all parts of my body. There weren't that many ripe peaches, having picked a lot yesterday, while walking towards the woods, knowing it was going to be quick. I'd make sure my underwear is underneath my ball-sack, helping when the pressure builds, adding extra seconds in the place I want to be, a place where I can't think about anything, doing anything to prolong not being in reality.

The sun was at three quarters, my energy much less, waiting for the distant rumble. None came, meandering through the trees, mind swirling from Dan to Jessie, struggling to find peace.

I needed to understand Dan. That is what I told myself! Try to understand beyond his frustration of too many bills and a sick wife. When I asked questions, however, he's always evasive. Who were the two boys next to the girl in the photograph on the mantle? The girl I assumed was Martha, together they looked like siblings. The handsome young man in the other photograph was Dan after studying every inch. It was taken while he was in Korea, confirming that when confronted, but that was all. Not even a rank or regiment. That was Dan's problem, he didn't want to talk about it, or anything. I guess he was taught not to have emotions and those that arise are to be ignored. It was after all what my father was trying to teach me every time he beat me.

IT'S ALL ABOUT MARTHA

I have no interest in anything God says, but quick to thank if something goes right, hearing what I wanted. There was no time to think, panting as I reached the farmhouse, the pickup starting up the lane. Dan wasn't alone in the car, Martha aside. Her head lay back, mouth open.

Dan called out the window. "John. Give me a hand," hopping out, racing to Martha's door. I was right behind.

I forgot all my problems offering Martha support, getting her steadied. This was not about me, nor Dan. It was about Martha, a separate living soul. Dan's demeanor was calm, which made me calm.

Martha looked frail, grey and unless mistaken had lost weight. Her hair wiry, frizzy and unwashed, eyes showing limited life.

Dan gave more orders. "I've got her, get the bags."

Martha made small, semi-independent steps to the farmhouse, following patiently behind, watching them united.

Dan laid her to rest, on her spot, in their bed. I put Martha's things in the corner departing to give them privacy. Dan wasn't done yet. "Get me a basin of hot water and soap," immediately doing as he said.

We had little to eat, that was ready. It wasn't like I knew how to cook, but enough to realize if vegetables and potatoes went in a pot we'd get somewhere. It struck me to get a bird, within minutes its neck was broken, feet off, feathers disappearing. This wasn't a difficult task spending many a week at a turkey farm getting them ready for Thanksgiving. Meat processing is the one part-time job a rural boy can rely on and I did.

Dan walked into the kitchen, not interested in him, my concern was for Martha.

"How is she?"

His face looked worried. "She wanted to come home, despite Doc saying no."

"I'm sorry," is all I could muster, looking at each other bewildered by the circumstance. He looked at the pot. "Smells good."

'Thanks, needs a bit and not done with my chores', is what I thought but didn't say it. He wasn't deserving of more comment than necessary. Despite the pleasant manner there was no way I was going to catch his eye. The day wasn't over, considering Dan a complication thus, to be avoided, walking out the kitchen head down.

The sun began to pitch sitting just above the hills, dark clouds blotted clear skies behind, the breeze increased. It was going to storm, ozone permeating the air, getting the cows sorted before the downpour, not wanting to make life more difficult than it is.

Returning the heavens were dark, thunder cracked, lightning bolts zigzagged across the sky. Fat droplets crashed onto to the dusty earth, air spicy, satisfying and a welcome reprieve from the heat.

Dan sat in his chair, staring straight ahead, looking drained.

"It's raining."

"I ain't deaf boy," his eyes not moving.

This didn't bother me, it was fair, my comment superfluous hoping the sweet, smell of my stew signaled we could eat. I looked in the pot and selected some of each ingredient, taking it to Dan.

"This is for Martha," presenting it to him, a simple offering of hope, as if the plate of food would change everything.

Dan stood up trying to catch my eye, my head down in a subservient manner, thinking 'take the food'. Doesn't he remember the other night?

"Thank you! I need you more than ever," touching me briefly on the shoulder, not expecting this response, warmth radiating through my body. Why did every interaction with him, no matter how small always amplified emotion? I hated him now, but still wanted him to make me feel secure, guide me. The contradiction hurts, the emotional instability hurts.

I brought the pot out to coincide with his descending footsteps. We ate in silence, the nutrition bringing us back to life. The food certainly helped my mood.

"You did good, real good."

I didn't need the compliment. If we were going to talk I'd ask burgeoning questions.

"Martha been sick for a while?"

"Yeah, been getting worse."

My concern for Martha was larger than his answer. "Can't they do anything for her?"

"Nope."

This monosyllabic response was frustrating but at the same time final, defining the situation. It was numbing, my response ladling more stew into his bowl. Automatically he ate it.

I went to bed laying out a plan for the next day on what needed to be done, letting Dan tend to his ailing spouse. I welcomed Dan and Martha needed me, liked being wanted and appreciated. It was all I ever asked.

***

In the early hours, Dan and Martha conversed, voices raised. Martha counteracting Dan's arguments for her to lay in bed.

"It's alright I feel fine, they said I should do a little. It'll do me good." Martha surprisingly sprite. Dan grunted, perhaps knowing his pleas were pointless.

I agreed with Martha. It made no sense for her to sit and wilt as nature apparently intended, also wanting to challenge his decision. "Good morning Martha. Glad to see you're feeling better, beautiful day outside."

It certainly was after the rain, Dan giving me a sharp look.

The cows were glad to see me. Was it my imagination they were smiling when I opened the gate? Naming each animal is not a habit of any true farmer, but I was happy that morning swinging on the fence singing silly songs. I knew why- everything was back to normal, even for a little while, like those fleeting first few days, knowing it wasn't going to last and trying to enjoy every minute.

80

***

My stomach churned after eating half a dozen over ripe peaches I didn't want Dan to find, having to go inside and shit preferably without the world hearing me.

Martha finished a much-needed batch of bread, Dan making a terrible effort at organizing the affair doing nothing but irritating the lady. She was pleasant, joyous and upon recollection, for the first time.

"Ya, made a great stew last night, prefer mine cooked longer, but very nice." Martha very nearly smiling. "Ready for some lunch?"

"Yes thanks."

We sat down to potatoes, small carrots, onions, interspersed with chunks of fatty pork. Lunch wasn't what I expected as Martha continued her spree of joy, while Dan sank deeper into bewilderment, melancholy smeared all over his face like a random artwork.

Martha and I chatted. Dan's focus swung from his wife to me, back to his wife, head acting as a pendulum, eventually standing up, marching out the room, arms folded. Now I had a chance.

"Mrs. Adams I would really like to write a letter to my girlfriend, Jessie I miss her so much," over-acting, enough to get her sympathy.

She attempted to move.

"No, let me," I said quickly, Martha pointing to the bureau. The writing material was in a leather-bound folder, initialed M.B, in a portion of the drawer that I never got to being distracted by all their bills. I folded the paper, tucked it in the envelope, placing the stamp inside.

Dan had worked out his problem marching back, quickly sitting and slipping the envelope into my shirt in one motion. His capture when entering, was me sitting next to Martha, arm around her shoulder and that is what I wanted him to see.

"Are you alright," asking Martha, expecting a smile in return, but no. I said it loudly pretending I was checking on her, but she wasn't. The color of her skin changing to a translucent puce. Martha fading from food and excitement made me feel guilty with a goal, admittedly unconscious until the last minute, to suit my purpose. Before I knew it, she was begging for help, Dan aiding her upstairs, face white and gasping for air.

Dan's look was fierce, blinding black bolts of anger shot out his eyes, aggression carrying Martha up the remaining stairs.

I planned on clearing the plates making a quick exit to the orchards. While rinsing the last of the dishes Dan galloped downstairs, too late. He looked unhappy, same face I'd seen the other night, instantly making my blood run cold. I observed him from head to toe, forehead pinched, eyes had no emotion, lips tense, hands fisted, backing off nearly dropping the last plate fearing an onslaught. I was sure Martha wanted one more day at home, doing what she's always done.

"I need to see you."

"It's what Martha wanted," justifying myself.

Dan sensed something, softening, always dialed in, a voice much gentler. "Come, let's go down to the cellar."

I didn't know there was one.

As told my experiences with older males in cellars was not good creating emotional havoc, similar to that of a barn, but much worse. We went outside. He lifted a series of wooden slats that I assumed was something else and below a set of uneven stairs.

I had no idea why I was following him, reminiscent of times Pa told me to follow him. Ma knew it happened. The day wire cables crisscrossed my back, creating bloody zigzags, I screamed so loud even God heard. Even though I loved my Ma, it's the one thing I hated her for, -she *never* said anything. However, in her life, or even our lives this was normal, and I was always too proud to show her exactly how much Pa hurt me.

This is what a person does when they are dominated by another. It doesn't matter how many warning signs there are, one just follows the same way a cow follows the one in front before electrocution, taking steps towards the new, double-lock door, horizon slowly disappearing. Why was I following him? -it's hardly surprising human imagination invented zombies.

The cellar was dusty, old tools scattered with spiders, witnesses to ungodly tales. Their webs manifestations of spirits who never made it to heaven. Musky from the rain, trickles of water mingled with dust to form little muddy rivers, like dark blood flowing from a freshly slain victim. My heart pounded staring at him, but he was himself, smile beaming. An affable man stood before me and not one about to attack.

"You're doing good John."

I gulped, internally embarrassed for letting my imagination run away. But it's not only me, it's common. It's what minds do with no place to go.

"We're gonna need more of that good cookin'. If you need meat there's plenty." Dan opening a large, pristine, white freezer which lay incongruously in this decaying space. I looked at Dan, then in the freezer, each piece of meat marked in a fastidiously.

"Thanks, yeah… that's great." My reality check coming in, shoving my hands deep in my pockets.

Dan's eyes steadied, "Martha wants to see you. Don't stay too long, then get your ass into the orchards."

I initially nodded but my curiosity took over, turning, eyebrows raised, "What about?"

"I don't know for God's sake," kicking the freezer. "Wants to tell you how to cook. What do I care?"

I irritated him unnecessarily, the reaction I blamed on myself. He had been gracious.

Martha's covers tossed aside, buxom she filled the night-gown, modestly fringed with lace, I approached. Initially she appeared asleep, eyes springing open, raspy, a ramble.

"John, it's good to see you. I like you very much, you're a nice boy…going to be a good man, I can tell," breathing heavily, struggling as the afternoon temperature rose.

"You wanted to give me some pointers," I said.

"Pointers?" Martha confused.

"On cooking, now you're sick?"

The smirk across her face indicated my lack of understanding of life, her marriage and especially her husband.

"Oh no…. you know how to cook. I know that…thank you for the soup, it made me feel better," speaking slowly, eyes suddenly lit, a flashback of a distant, unknown memory. Sighing, "You know we never had children?"

"Yes."

"We've always needed a young man, like yourself, sometimes two, to help us in the summer… it's all too much for us."

"Yes," not understanding the conversation.

"My husband is a good man…he likes you… he always does."

Martha was trying to tell me something.

"I like you, more than the others, can see it in your eyes, you've been… many times. I don't want you…"

I didn't understand the two words she swallowed while trying to gain oxygen. The missing words I'd figure out, but the incriminating words were, 'more than the others'.

I was shocked, speechless, surprised, Martha confirmed what sat firmly in the back of my head. Politely put, it was not Dan's first rodeo. Martha's words struck home, leaving me stranded on a tiny emotional island riddled with sour fruit, above a burning sun scorching my skin.

I thought about the other boys and how far he got with them. The so-called boyish antics by the pond and subsequent sexual encounter was what? - Yeah, another day in my life of Daniel Adams.

I pulled peach after peach, one more angrily than the other, dignity preventing me from smashing them. That would only annoy him, even though temporarily satisfying, but far from my intention, questioning the person I was dealing with. The answer was clear. I was nothing but tasty morsel and another game for Dan and for that matter Jessie. I the double fool. One male, one female, they both had me.

Figures of that man and woman rose up like a multi-headed serpent each trying to draw me in. I kneeled on the floor diminished in sweet subservience letting them, or their surrogates, exercise passion or pain as they wished. My manhood stripped I'd crawl and do anything they say. The bushel slipped, ten perfect peaches falling to the ground.

***

With vegetables from the garden, and a piece of roasted meat from the freezer, Dan took a plate upstairs for Martha, waiting before eating, wanting to show I was better than him. I served, refusing to engage in conversation. Talking would recognize his licentious nature. Dan couldn't stand the silence.

"Thanks John, this is good." Helping himself to a second plate.

The compliment wasn't enough for me, sitting arms folded waiting for him to finish.

"Martha must have given you some good tips." He smiled and wish he didn't, face alive, charisma oozing like a metaphysical mass but didn't want to be fooled.

"You Okay?"

I just nodded.

Dan's face went from friendly to tense. "No you're not. I can tell."

"It's nothing."

"Can't be nothing, if you're looking like this. You're lying to me!"

"Just tired. I'm going to bed."

I disregarded cleaning the table starting towards my room, then came the command.

"Get back down here."

There was so much in my head it was a lottery of what I'd say. All the balls bubbled in that big airy machine of my brain. One floated-by which I couldn't quite catch, not being able to articulate the problem. Then another, a bright red ball with, 'you're a slut' written on it. Oh no! It's the letter "J".

Secretly I wanted to talk through my problems with someone and without judgment. Who wouldn't? - things get a lot clearer. That's why psyches are like the old telephone booth except a lot more expensive.

Despite telling myself time and time again Dan shouldn't know, telling is a mistake, I blubbered every detail. What I did to Jessie, how I must apologize, say I love her when I don't, all in the hope Jessie, and thus her brothers and father will forgive me.

This is the wicked part of being vulnerable wanting Dan to feel sorry for me. I struggled to please him through work, everything, but still wanted to connect. Telling him will bring us closer. This was also my jealousy, the sense of being cheated, trying to make a compromise for possible additional emotional space in his world. I would never care about my predecessor's if I was the one he chose. When it came time to leave he'd understand I had no place to go, catching me at the last minute looking into my teary eyes saying, 'Son why don't you stick around.' Then I wouldn't have to go home. I'd find myself a girlfriend and Dan would be my Pa.

I didn't realize it while explaining my sordid problems, including the possibility I could never go home, ended up handing over all information he needed. Dan showed a twisted form of empathy, calculated, coming closer and closer, picking me up firmly in his arms instantly taking control of my emotions, commanding me to believe in his false love.

"Boy, don't worry."

His heart laughing all the way to the bank.

"I just need a little help," beginning to sob.

"My boy ain't gonna worry."

Trusting him again, believing there was security in his arms and household, officially forgiving him for throttling me and his other 'actions'. I was wrong anyway, that was Martha's spot. And what the fuck did I expect?...that he never looked at a boy's ass on a hot day, blood doing double time in *all* parts of his body.

"Yes," getting that feeling again, my nose nestled in his neck.

From a distance this was an embrace of father to son, the caption, 'I love you son. I'm proud of you son'. For me it is happening, soul repair lasting for five seconds, before Dan pushed me back, shaking me from my dreamy state.

He gave advice, but I needed convincing.

"Do you really love her son?" His face upright, looking at each other as men should.

"I don't know," I said truthfully, because that is what I would have said to a real Pa.

"Oh son, don't get ya heart stuck on one soul. Time and fate will bring the right one," Dan paused, sighing regretfully, "…with no time gone. You can't be there yet."

I was so confused, impossible to define any single emotion, all life's demons rearing their head at once.

"Give it your best shot, not too slushy now." Dan laughing as I went upstairs.

I knew strapping chains around a wrenching and wrestling heart was wrong as I wrote.

Dear Jessie,

You are always in my dreams.

What happened the night I left was not like me. We are together two years and I've always respected you. This is between me and you, we can work it out, love has it ways.

I will see you soon Jessie. I'm busy many hours of the day but think of you the whole time. Forgive me Jessie, let's put this behind us.

I'm looking forward to seeing you in the Fall. I think about you every day.

I love you.

John

It was all I could write. The little black devil on my shoulder reminded me I wasn't the first guy to say, 'I love you', simply to get out of trouble. After talking to Dan, the faux 'I love you', didn't mean a thing. Nothing to be sorry about son, happens all the time. Dan and the little black devil were one. That letter got me into a lot of trouble.

***

Sunday rolled around and we were heading to church. Martha hadn't left her bed in days deciding to pray for her. My prayer is going to make me feel better and not Martha.

That's what prayers do, make you feel like a good person, an egotistical exercise thus pointless.

I hadn't been speaking to Dan because I revealed too much of myself the other night. I was quiet, wondering about everything, it slowly sinking in how stupid it was telling him everything. I felt he knew more about me than I of him, feeling exposed.

Dan broke the silence. "Listen, John you have a problem. I know. You're doing a great job now Martha is sick, but you're acting mighty strange. Ya might wanna remember who's house it is."

This was a reference to me making an omelet when he wanted fried eggs, or worse, casually walking to collect his paper while he seethed on the porch. Also 'Dan from the other night' hadn't been around much, being mostly gnarly, which in this case I did put down to Martha, his anger more frustration than actual hatred.

The real answer to his question was part of me still wanted him back, and acting up in my juvenile brain, was the solution. A man doesn't really have a head on his shoulders until twenty-three and considering my upbringing I was behind.

Dan didn't know what my problem was, because I didn't know what my problem was. Infatuation isn't a rational feeling or process, which in part created and explains my silence. Its continuance is guaranteed by intrigue, fueled by underlying jealousy, which didn't want to go away, thinking I've solved this problem. But jealousy isn't like that, always going to dominate thought until full explanation is provided.

Blurting it out, "You have a farm hand every year?"

"Need one every year, yeah! Why?"

My stare piercing and knowing distracting him from driving, the vehicle swinging into the opposite lane.

"… maybe this explains why you've been on the quiet side," under his breath.

"So, this happens every year?" I wanted to hear him say it.

"Why do you think that?...", pausing before, "…and no…. no. This doesn't happen every year and never like this."

This wasn't a lie, now believing he would have made deeper inroads, but the grooming schedule was delayed due to Martha's illness.

"What do you mean?" My teeth grinding.

Dan pulled to the side of the road.

One hand was on the steering wheel and the other on my leg bringing his face closer. "I mean that you took me by surprise and made a lot of stuff feel good."

I swear that's a line from a movie, couldn't look at him in the face, reluctant to meet his gaze.

"Common John look at me," semi-pleading.

I did as he said, having to. His eyes shot out green flecks, they were deep, moist with emotion, reaching out putting his hand on my shoulder in an acknowledgment that it was okay. Now I felt good again.

"That's my boy. Why don't you go to the pond, spend the afternoon up there. I'll see Martha gets what she needs?"

This gesture of free time was much needed, tired, days had been long, thinking of the cool water, how I'd sink into the depths and disappear from the world. Deep water, another of my escape methods from reality, you don't think about life without oxygen.

***

After church Simon and I mulled our thoughts under the cherry tree which brimmed with fruit we weren't allowed to touch.

There was an expectation you spoke with your own group, the men in charge, the older men, women making the men in charge do what they should, the older women, boys wanting to talk to girls and finally the farmhands.

Most families were prepared for the long summer season with strapping work-age sons and daughters, some had cousins helping. There was just the two of us who didn't fit in, confirmed by another rejection from Mary Ann and Mary Beth. I pretended not to care but hate rejection, preferring a whack in the balls.

They didn't want us to talk to them, and after consideration wasn't so sure how much I cared. They could go as cardboard robots on Halloween with little adjustment, comparing them to my attentive friend. A human who doesn't scorn, sneer or laugh in your face.

We stood close, Simon and I on one side of the tree, the two girls on the other, my eyes dancing between them. Simon wasn't looking at the girls but at me.

Simon couldn't explain it and I didn't want him too, now accepting it was normal for his eyes to survey my teddy body. I liked the ways his eyes picked out my features; pecs, thighs, smile or even when he looked at my bulge a little too long. It was warming, more a sign we were getting comfortable around each other, or more accurately, me with him. He liked me and I wanted to be liked. Now when we met, it was, 'Hey buddy'.

Visually Simon was not the kind of guy I was used to seeing. Everyone I knew was as big, or bigger than me. Simon would stick out like a sore thumb in Medford, picked on endlessly, wondering if that is true where he came from but couldn't ask.

"Si, how many in your family did you say?"

"I don't know, a couple of hundred all told."

I laughed, "Ah that's funny, sounds like you're all related."

"Considering we keep to ourselves. We probably are!"

His intellect consistently challenged me, and superior wit made him more than an equal. It was difficult not to visually like him either with a naturally caring, face consistently happy.

"You comin' up this afternoon."

"Wish I could we're goin' out."

"You get out?"

I was happy for him, of course, a little jealous but in this case in a nice way, approaching instinctively.

"Yeah, we take the girls all sorts of places. I know the area quite well."

Simon should learn to change his tone of voice while boasting, sounding irritating, letting it wash over me, smiling, oddly wanting to get even closer.

I saw him out the corner of my eye, but it was too late.

"You boys ain't normal. You should be looking at those girls instead of each other." The Sherriff said a little too loudly, standing boldly hands on hips, expression smug. How I fucking hate smug? No, you don't have the right look at me like that, expression predetermined, mind made up, looking all his fingers. No gold ring where it should be. You want me to make a conclusion about that? It works both ways.

"We're talking and not wishing to disturb others." Simon stating exactly what the Sherriff just did, with enough volume for defense, warning off the person who I was more than uneasy about. Simon defended me, Sheriff moving on, lifting his nose towards a savory source, fortunately fixated on food.

***

It was the short period Dan and I lived in relative harmony. Harmony assuming, I did everything he said promptly without question. I remained on the receiving end of frequent barks which I saw as pain from his ailing wife, again. When he got angry, it was mostly about work.

When the day was done, we hung in clean T's and shorts, space smelling of soap, never long, maybe an hour or so before bed. We eyed each other every five or ten minutes. Dan being a scratcher, junk never truly comfortable, was initially interesting, but now I'd gotten used to it. In fact, it was irritating since watching him scratch made me want to.

I respected Dan like a son should a respect a Pa, making me work hard, a case of treat 'em mean keep them keen'. It wasn't great but I understood it, certainly no one or two dollar bonuses, which I put down to debt.

I started reflecting on the possible number of Dan's lies or misrepresentations. The pond wasn't entirely his. He and Mr. Stenton built it together, modernizing an antiquated irrigation system. He didn't lie about full ownership of the new pick-up, nor the milk equipment but certainly made me believe it owned it and he was a huge success. He even lied about the create of beer at the bottom of the pond, it was Stenton's. Dan never purchased any beer, only whiskey.

Days ticked past, Martha lay in bed, bowls sent up and down. Sometimes their door was open, resisting asking, 'How are you?'

FIRST CONTACT

It was another Sunday, my clumsy hairy beefcake body next to Simon's elegant figure, laying on vivid verge next to the crystal-clear pond, would have fascinated Hockney, Seurat and beyond, all wanting to paint this scene.

Simon reflected. "You mind if Mary Ann is?" Making the shape of a curvaceous women in the air.

"You mean big," cutting to the chase.

It was a stupid question and why he asked is another. At my age any vagina is a good vagina, even if pus oozes ten days later. I thought about three things; Dan, Jessie, and sex. Except sex came first, not unlike any other young man. Simon was also a young man, yet imagining him with a woman was difficult and that's not out of disrespect.

Simon was in the woods earlier. I was on my way to my favorite tree after Dan yelled at me for nothing, drinking when we got home from church, losing control. I fed him, everything clean, nothing to complain about. Frustrated I marched past the initial brush to the sound of rustling leaves, someone running away. It could only have been Simon. I didn't go to my tree, feelings of guilt sweeping through my body, not from wasting sperm but because I had other, updated feelings.

Mind awry, body expecting something sexual, forced me into the water. Simon sitting up, observing.

Imagining I was in my natural habitat, somewhere in Alaska, feasting on salmon, made the water pay, thumping the surface until my mind was blank, open and ready. I thought about how kind Simon was while sitting at the bottom of the pond, surrounded by brown plants that still survive in this depth. How he paid so much attention to Stenton's kids, to everyone. All the ladies loved him which wasn't true for me.

I walked out the pond, goose-bumps popping up, seeing no reason to feeling cold when there was no breeze, hot air all around from a blazing sun.

"What's up?" Simon turning to his side, lifting his left leg over the other, trying to hide his penis previously reminiscent of cooked squiggly pasta but now proud and twitching. I didn't blame him; it's why I went swimming.

Kinda knew why I said it. Yes, Simon was all I got, but he was a smart fuck and had my attention.

"You Okay there?" I muttered as there was no way for him to hide what was happening, fully engorged was still skinny and long, foreskin over the end, wanting to pull it back and watch his cock-head pop out. I owed him one, accessing my fascination, deciding there was no technical or emotional reason not to.

Previous expectations meant living up to Dan's. I hate expectations and for that matter assumptions. Dan expected me to suck him off like a whore and assumed I could. Simon assumed he would get a good look at my cock while I took a nap, essentially expecting nothing. Simon also assumed I was the straight dude whom he should look up to and not the same vulnerable, loving creature in a different animal suit. He presumed I had no feelings for him and that wasn't true. It's why I changed my plans for my date with the oak tree.

Moving on my side it was obvious we were both ready. The question was, what is next? Who will make the first move? I was open to touching, if he wanted to go down, I'd let him, but that is also what I wanted. Softer would be nicer, certainly not Dan's way, open to tasting and feeling his personal textures on my lips and tongue.

When I asked Simon, 'You Okay there', it was an open question, positioning myself, inching my body closer, catching his gaze, movements prehistoric not wanting to show all my hand.

My cock, with the ups and downs of the day, didn't have long to go before it would be over. Simon responded, leaking, bouncing on his stomach as he flexed his glutes rhythmically, beginning to think he didn't need me to touch him.

He did caress himself once, but barely. I wanted to reach over and jerk him while he did mine, together we'll bust, it'll be over. All tension released.

It would be up to me to lead the way, decision made.

"Hey, buddy," was all I said, reaching over gently touching his shaft initially with just one finger. Simon instantly tightly shut his eyes pretending this wasn't happening as I began the massage, his teeth clenched. Simon groaned, my hand quickly sticky, cock slipping in and out of my fat-fingered-fist.

Simon was left to fantasize while I worked his cock, important factors which make up a

bro-job. He deserved it, not only to repay for what I did on our first meeting, but wanted to play my way and with someone I could trust.

Apart from sounds of Simon's panting and his penis being masturbated I didn't hear anything, concentrating on his forthcoming climax, imagining what it will be like. If an F-4 Phantom flew over I wouldn't have heard anything, certainly not Dan.

He shouted at the top of his lungs...getting closer. Come on Simon, there were seconds left before he'd see us. I panicked, spat on my finger shoving it inside him, middle digit disappearing with ease, Simon semi-squealed. The spew started almost instantly, ropey before tightening my grip. I wanted my bro to blow his mind as well as his cock. The pressure too much, Simon signaling, shots bombarding his stomach, smelling it and liking it.

I got my underwear on in time to hide my remaining boner, a shot of adrenalin is worse than kryptonite and can whip the stiffness out of anything. Simon turned onto his stomach hiding the evidence.

"John," Dan scaling the mound. I don't get it, why my respect name? His head and shoulders in sight, something was wrong, seriously wrong.

"Are you deaf?"

Then I knew exactly what it was, pulling up my pants, buttoning my shirt calling back.

"Sorry I was asleep."

Dan's motion was disturbing, arms above his head, staggering. The only time I ever saw him breathless. There was no point saying anything, trying to hug him, Dan's fists beating my back, whimpering, "Martha".

My own sense of loss was irrelevant. Even though working hard, this was the day when the work really began, needing to support Dan, somehow. What could I do? - now in an embrace, Dan continuing to breathe deeply, eyes pointed to the heavens extending his jaw, puffy cheeks and tears catching the sunlight.

Slowly he checked himself, relaxing his shoulders, making a point of catching his gaze. His eyes were misty, couldn't read them, empty. I've seen joy, knowledge, anger and the devil but they were vacant, his body soulless. I told myself his soul temporarily left his body to catch up with Martha's. It was time to take control.

"Dan!" Shaking him, "Come let's go."

"No."

Dan wasn't ready to deal with it.

"I will help you," holding his scaly hand.

Without an answer we made our way back, walking closely, the time speechless.

The front door creaked, as did the floors, staircase, and finally the hallway standing at the entrance to their bedroom. Martha's eyes were open, hair flung, left hand over her shoulder, looking awkward, uncomfortable and not peaceful. The room predominately smelled of human waste; for some reason the window was shut.

Dan shuffled, voice deeper than normal. "Take the keys…call the doctor… go to the church." Orders coming out in bits.

I ran downstairs, took the keys from the dresser and was on my way without a conscious thought. Then it set in, guts churning. What was going to happen? The image of her dead body, the stench, wintery colors, the feeling you are being watched by a soul trying to dissipate. It all flooded back, gulping, esophagus filling, choking not accepting this was happening, swerving while opening the car door, head hung, my stomach's contents steaming on hot asphalt.

There was no time to think, slamming the door, hitting the accelerator, acid corroding my throat and mouth. I was focused on what was in front, and not anything behind. In my rear-view mirror several tons of metal charged, about to ram, screeching rubber bringing the looming semi to my attention. I slammed the gas, and with a miracle the pickup leaped forward, changing gears to the tune of a blaring horn. The driver's skill meant I didn't end up a tidy wreck. Rightfully he flashed his headlights, held out a strong arm, a fist, and a middle finger.

Benton was simple, one main street, one cross street, the gas station on the corner, pulling up to the phone.

The doctor was silent for the first part of the conversation, my words ejaculating in random spasms. The monotone response pacified me. He'll be on his way as soon as possible.

The church was not a mile away. The cool breeze keeping me calm heading to the Pastor's house. It was late afternoon, the man waking-up from a nap as I burst in blurting the news, speech patterns agitated.

The Pastor far from his youth made a quick recovery, ordering me to sit in a large hunchbacked chair while calling his wife. "Get this boy some lemonade or something, he's losing his mind," turning, reassuring me, "It's gonna be alright boy."

"What boy?" The Pastors' wife marched in, armed with apron and opinion. "Oh, that boy," pretending my sight made her sick.

"It's Mrs. Adams, she's passed."

"I'm sorry to hear that, poor women most likely worried herself to death. God bless her soul." Her face sculptured in sanctity sent a signal. The women swooped down like a hawk attacking prey as she snapped, "It would have been different if he wasn't ..."

"That's enough Sybil, we are all upset," the Pastor interrupted.

I only wanted to hear, 'Everything was going to be alright,' and certainly not her animosity.

She did her duty delivering delicious crisp cold lemonade. On the phone she covered the mouthpiece, wanting to go home. Immediately after the handset was replaced, got up offering my hand in appreciation. He accepted the gesture gracefully, wife scurried to the corner, fists clenched.

I slowed down the ride home, barely pushing the gas, wondering what I'd find at the farmhouse. The sun hung like a globule of gold melting behind the hills diffusing a myriad of colors, knowing it would be all gone in a few minutes.

***

No exterior lights were on, none on the inside. The silence was odd, not a sound, night creatures having nothing to say, stoically taking one stair at a time. It didn't matter what was going to happen, no way of controlling it, like the sun melting behind the hills, switching on the hall light, their bedroom door slightly ajar.

"Dan," pushing the door open, slowly illuminating the room. He lay next to his wife clutching her folded hands, every detail in perfect clarity unforgettable. The living spending last moments with the deceased. No one could disturb this scene, especially not me, their intimacy, summation of life, to physical, to personal, pushing me away.

I prepared food; chopping, mixing, frying, all shielding me from the outside world, creating life where there was none. People would be arriving, having something to offer was expected. Quickly cornbread was in the oven. I'd left stew meat in the refrigerator, watery blood collecting at the bottom of the bowl, death all around me. This animal died, there is always death before dinner.

I wanted the smell of frying meat to permeate the house having to reinforce life goes on. Not for Dan's sake but mine. I was upset by Martha's death and struck by what I saw. Dan spent the last hours lying next to Martha, paralyzed, grief touching the surface. If only he knew how deep it would sink in.

Bringing life to this house would mean life might re-enter Dan, tossing in fresh tomatoes, a can of beans and ample hot sauce covering the skillet.

There was no sound from upstairs, trying to sit down, becoming impatient wanting whomever to arrive. Anxiety kicked in, beginning with a pinch behind my jaw, then the top of my throat turning into a self- imposed semi strangulation that I can't control.

I cleaned spilled blood in the fridge, pots and surfaces, disappearing into my own special world of unadulterated fantasy. Anything to distract myself. I was an airline pilot, a judge, a bank manager, a scientist, going through all professions. Imaging myself in the uniform, my wife next to me and our kids. Jessie was not in any of them. My wife was a brunette and a nurse.

I didn't hear the vehicle approach, too deep in thought, footsteps marching in the living room. Two ladies appeared, looked at me tensely, apparently not impressed with anything and especially my stew.

One lady spoke. "God bless Martha." They looked the same; small, wide shouldered, big bottomed, hair in a bun, puffy-pink cheeks with frills on their dresses and aprons to remind everyone they were feminine.

"We'll need hot water." The younger one said.

"In the sink," pointing at the tap.

"…and a wash bowl," they said together.

I needed to warn Dan. The ladies filled the kitchen, skirting around their rotund figures was not easy, pressing against bosom and buttock.

"Over there." Pointing to a shelf.

Dr. Strauss stood near the dining room table. He was a very, tall figure, below average muscles needing physical work, classic of those who think too much. He had a full head of hair which complemented the boyish expression. Any illusion of youth or even joviality was short lived, as his spoken words were thoughtless and dismissive.

"Who are you?" He questioned.

"We spoke on the phone. I'll get Mr. Adams. Please wait here," not going to be intimidated, brushing past him.

Dan sat on the edge of the bed; face filled with grief.

99

I whispered. "Everyone's here."

He remained motionless not seeming to care. I touched his shoulder, body not moving, decided to make it clear.

"Everyone's here. Let me help you!"

Dan didn't say anything. I gripped his upper arm, then don't know why, but buried my head into his neck and waited. After a while and no response loosened my grip on his arm to rub his back. Eventually he put hands on his knees gradually rising. He walked slowly, several seconds between steps, made the stairs seem like an obstacle course before plunging into his chair.

I poured him a large glass of whiskey, while the doctor and two ladies went upstairs.

The doctor was back within minutes, expressionless, handing Dan a piece of paper. "These are hard, trying times, no doubt. She was a fine woman."

"John, get Doc a drink and something good." Dan's voice faint, hoarse and an octave higher than normal.

Dr. Strauss said. "Kid! Get him a bowl as well."

Despite being an asshole, doc was apparently good at his job noticing the beginning of a long, slow, painful, degradation of Daniel Adams, seemingly wanting to delay that with food.

I didn't think of myself as a kid, but left the burner on high. In another minute it would have been crispy stew, and maybe doc would have been right.

The volume in the living room rose, boots, an offer of deepest sympathies. In Dan's bowl I put less concentrating on navigating Dr. Strauss's bowl, which I filled to the brim, probably thinking this is the way to treat a guest.

The bull of a Sherriff was the third man. I have nothing to fear of law enforcement, but he automatically makes me feel nervous, inferior and guilty of something, spilling some of Dr. Strauss's stew on the floor. The Sheriff looked at me in disgust, hands on hips, one hand close to handcuffs, other inches from a firearm.

Dr. Strauss took the bowl, instantly asking for a cloth to wipe his hands, while Dan tried to swipe his away. I fetched for the doctor, then a drink for the bull who reminded me what I was doing.

"What the fuck boy?" The Sherriff gazing at my stewey footsteps across the hardwood floors.

I got on my hands and knees, all three men looking at me, observing my desperate wipes to clean. The towel was absorbent but left a glossy, fatty film.

"Boy, you're shit at this." The Sheriff complained.

"He's all I got, Silas." Dan was losing his voice.

"Drink some of that my friend, it'll soothe your throat. What you say doc?" The Sherriff said, pouring more whiskey.

"Better than anything I got for...," musing in that unnecessary professorial way, "for a sore throat," all laughing. It wasn't funny.

The Sherriff has a real name, Silas. A name meant for good men, lords of ecology, harmony, green, my favorite color and not. "Don't spill it this time, fuck boy."

I thought of poisoning the food. It would be fitting to see this Goliath brought down by something insidious, a creeping chemical culminating in death.

Silas would do anything, using his place of power, for pleasure and gain. In his presence my muscles ached from his aura, hearing shrill sounds of desperate souls, shouting, 'Please no, no.' I was humble, pretending to be grateful giving him this meal, and truly was hearing the approaching car, realizing I'd might be spared from further humiliation.

"They're here," Dan said.

Two tall well-dressed men got out of a long, black car, thinking it was going to be difficult to get Mrs. Adams down the stairs. Certainly, a good time to disappear, but the doctor caught my arm.

"You might have to help," handing me his glass graciously, but shoved his bowl into my chest, spilling the remainder on my shirt, smiling. "Dan, I'm on my way. Sorry for your loss, maybe for the best. You can do what you want now."

The Doc was confident, knowing all about the world and why it worked, the condescending wink directed towards me proving that. The Sherriff chuckled observing my every move like a true creep.

Doc was almost out the door, before swiveling on his heals making a bee line back to me. I didn't think anything because I was scared, but he put his hand in his pocket pulling out some pills.

"Whatever the fuck your name is, make sure he takes one at breakfast for the next few days, especially before the funeral," slipping four blue pills into my hand.

One of the undertakers greeted Dan, and after a brief site survey went outside to confer with his buddy.

The stairs shook like an impending earthquake. The ladies were done.

The two men skillfully maneuvered the box through the living room and up the stairs. Would I get to see Mrs. Adams again? There was a thud, a short sound of something heavy falling, thinking there was no point in waiting, getting to the top of the stairs in an instant. The coffin was in the hall, Martha Adams inside, air smelled fresh, her skin looked clean. The men lifted the lid sealing it and she disappeared.

"You need help?" I called.

"Once she's downstairs you can," the taller and skinnier answered.

The sound of men heaving, and huffing ensued for several minutes, before their legs appeared at the top of the stairs. Step by step backwards, the first man descended.

"Get that table out the way." The second called, equipped with more muscle yet for something reason had the lighter end.

At a reachable point I joined in, trying to support the weight. Considering my youth, I'd be able to accept a considerable redistribution, arms held high, the coffin tilting.

"Watch what you're doing." The skinnier complained.

102

Chastised I continued with caution, and with minimal additional disturbance Mrs. Adams gradually made her way to the hearse and the back door slammed.

What Did I do Wrong?

I did see Martha again, three days later. I guessed Dan loved Martha in some way, no way of really knowing, but presumed she was intrinsic to his orbit. When carried away, Martha's physical presence imploded creating a black hole, the absence wreaking havoc in his mind.

Death creates a gap, an open space, a void, the essence of loss. The person is no longer there, life must re-populate that space before the bereaved become whole again. Until then, Dan was going to fill that space with alcohol. He started in the morning, was seriously drunk by lunch, slept, then did the whole thing again before bed.

Scared I worked hard, not wanting to give Dan's volatile character a reason to fluctuate, even trying to introduce the Doc's blue pills and failing. There was reason to base this on, as there are men and men on alcohol. Usually they aren't the same person, evident in my own father, taking lashings because that seemed like a fun thing to do at the time.

The days were filled with caution. I fed him, stayed close, but away, and when the time came got his clothes together for Martha's funeral.

I was worried from the start, still he stirred in his bedroom, followed by a short grunt and even a hum, indicating things would proceed without too many problems. The notion was quickly dismissed, Dan banging on my door.

He paced the living room, without speech. I crept my way to the kitchen, gave him coffee, then breakfast, without exchanging a word. Dan ate, first time I'd seen him consume anything of nourishment since Martha's death, thinking it appropriate to try again placing a pill next to his plate.

"What's that?'

"Doc said, don't you remember?"

"How many times have I told you," sneering, brushing the pill aside, making a dash for the cabinet that held his stash.

He swigged, seemed in a hurry, pacing the room like a lion in a circus arena. Some unknown force whipping his tortured soul, making him growl louder to scare the crowd. He looked like a guilty man, guilty of something, but whose to know as we all feel guilty after death. It's part of the grieving process.

It didn't matter as I had jobs to do, walking out to the early sun suspended above the hills, a fiery ball rising quickly in the sky. It scared me, again I couldn't stop it, could never stop it. The day would go on.

Dan was anxious and wanted to get this over, relating, hoping he would be relaxed, snoozing after his snifter and before the big event. Just not more drinking please.

I was wrong. He sat at the table, eggy plate pushed aside, tumbler half full, third of the bottle gone, wanting to calm him, somehow, simply not willing to allow alcohol to be the only solution.

"We're gonna do this." Making sure my grip was firm, not just a touch, beginning to knead my knuckles into his neck and shoulders. I merely wanted to support someone at their time of loss, as one human would do to another, forcefully pushing his head forward to define this was therapeutic.

I thought I 'loved' Dan, at some time, admittedly in a very simple way, but any 'love', even microbial, based on pity and infatuation is a fatal cocktail. The relationship was flawed, raw, like a wound and open to abuse. If only I knew it at the time, but I tried and tried again. I wanted to be that person somewhere between a son and a buddy. That's all, hoping at this time of crisis he'd appreciate me.

No one is saying that women don't support each other in times of crises, but traditionally men have done it well and usually more 24/7 than female chats. A man to man relationship depends on mental and physical exchanges. The mental means we are on the same wavelength, camaraderie, pulling grit until the job is done and relief at the bar, discovering it's not only your wife who doesn't like the taste of cum. Then there are physical needs meaning it's perfectly normal, at the end of the day, to beat each other's heads in. Nowadays, this is normally called sports; football, hockey or boxing, definitely not golf, unless you want to use the club to crack a bone. Apart from that, golf is not even a pastime, more like a waste of time and a waste of green space, its concept understandably upsetting to me.

I massaged harder, working up his neck muscles into weedy, fluffy hair that needed cutting, running my fingertips around his ears towards his temples. Dan sighed, a physical release of energy beginning with a guttural noise, back arched, eyes closed. On his temples, my index fingers started in small circles, increasing in radius, moving over his scalp, hands running from the top of his head to the base of his neck. Dan's vocal cords grinded from satisfying murmurs to sounds of instruments unknown.

He had been a puppet since I touched him. Limp in my hands gave me a feeling of power. Not a power I wanted to misuse but one which granted pleasure. I liked touching him, my mind wondered to massaging his hold body, fingers teasing away every sorrow and pain from his inner being.

"Hey, you're done," I said, loud and clear, mostly to shake myself from another imaginary state. Yet Dan wasn't 'done'. Far from it, with shaggy hair and a poor shave, certainly not ready to attend his wife's funeral. There were scissors and a razor in the bathroom and Dan would have to accept.

"Hey, look at all this." Grabbing chunks of sandy fluff. "This has got to go!"

The less I said the better, Dan not budging as I dashed to the bathroom. It hadn't been long, maybe a minute while I searched, another drink sitting before him.

I started combing and cutting before a change of mind, his and mine, locks tumbling down. Dan's head hung, scents of whiskey filled my nostrils combined with odorous sweat, breakdown products of alcohol exuding from his skin.

I shaved the back of his neck, sideburns, motioning him towards me to check my work. Dan's eyes opened. He looked good enough.

"You're done." Deep and clear. He didn't move so I motioned. "Common we'd better get there, and you need a shower."

Dan stood up defiantly, "Don't you think I know."

He spent five minutes in the bathroom reappearing in the clothes I laid out for him, swigged one last dash of whiskey tilting like the leaning tower, steadying himself, but not before crashing into the dining room table.

"Let's go boy."

It took a while for Dan to settle in the driver's seat, belching when turning the ignition. A gear was out, his head hitting the steering wheel as the pickup sprang unexpectantly forward. He looked up trying to focus but couldn't.

"Hey, why don't you sit here, I'll drive," gesturing.

Dan's eyes were vehement. "No."

The vehicle stuttered down the lane swinging onto the main road. Dan, like any drunk, does a great job for about a minute, long enough for the muscles in his eyes to tire and for luck to play out.

"Whoa man…let's...err," I said, Dan swerving, trying to become bolder, "Let me drive," irritated.

He didn't budge but eased off the gas, instead of breakneck speed the pickup meandered mostly on the wrong side. When reaching a crest in the road he looked the other way. After the third hillock it was over, an oncoming vehicle approaching, and Dan wasn't pulling over. I gripped the seat, freezing fear, looked at Dan several times, all my remarks indicating anger, stop and let me drive.

We avoided that vehicle and back on the right side of the road. Within seconds the pickup drifted on the opposite side again and there was the same problem, an oncoming car traveling at high speed.

"Dan, we have to be…" He wasn't even looking at the road. "Dan you're going to…" shouting!

Dan looked over at me, hands following suit, pickup swerving within feet of impact, horn blasting. Dan couldn't control the machine, no one could, it being best he was drunk letting it ride for a few seconds. If he jabbed the brakes we would have flipped and rolled around like a barrel falling off Niagara Falls. The Gods also gave some absolution as he yanked the steering wheel in the opposite direction at the right moment, skidding off the asphalt and into the verge. Dan's hand ran out thereafter, grappling the steering wheel in desperation. The last twist leaving the back wheels skidding, swinging 180 degrees, back end bouncing off a tree trunk, our untied bodies thrown to the side like a bumper car from hell.

I was trying to gain control. Time had stopped while the accident occurred and now it started again, my warp catching up to Dan, red-faced, fury firing all cylinders, anger rising.

All I said was. "Oh shit."

"Shut up, you fuck!"

Dan's clenched fists beat his thighs like warrior before battle, neck taught, eyes bulged, millions of scarlet capillaries bursting.

Dan lunged over, hand catching my shirt bringing my head down and proceeded with swift, hard, smacks across my face. Smack is a polite word giving him credit, more like desperate half punches from a man at the end of the road.

"Don't ever tell me what to do!"

The attack ensued, the initial shock made me forget the pain, head flipping from side to side, his hand swooping down, back and forth, my jaw aching.

He grabbed my hair, growling, "You fuck…who do you think you are?… uh!"

His left hand loosened the grip on my collar advancing to pinching the upper region of my neck, right hand taking another full, hard swipe.

He was pinching my arteries, hard, blood not going into my brain. This is not technically strangulation, but effective in turning someone blue before the lights go out and extremely painful, pressure in my cranium building. You want to yell from the pain, but you can't, it's weird.

"You come into my house, act like some Betty fucking Crocket…" His eyes popped so fucking big I swear they would burst. "…boss me around all morning and now you're telling me how to drive."

108

Dan held his hand in mid-air, looked at his fingers as if creating a sculpture, pointed them, before plunging three digits down my throat.

"You need to watch your mouth!"

I couldn't breathe but blood flooded into my brain, he couldn't do both. I gargled on his fingers which receded when he realized it would get messy, immediately starting to complain.

"I said shut the fuck up." The frenzy not receding.

Never knew what is best, fight back or let them take it out on me, eventually it stops. The passive philosophy predominated, but the violation continued. There was nothing else to do but fight, delivering a crushing hit to Dan's testicles with my elbow. Instinctively he crouched while I twisted his ears, yelling. "Get off me."

Dan grimaced, face tensed. "Mother fucker."

There was no waiting for him to stop. The fight would go on, or I could make one last desperate appeal for peace grabbing his collar, crying. "You need to stop."

Dan, either from hearing the shrill in my voice, or from the searing pain in his balls began to focus.

"Stop, fucking stop! You need to bury your wife," hoarse with exasperation.

It was the 'bury your wife' that made him back off. Dan's eyes welled with tears. He choked and convulsed from emotion, tears squirting and spewing from every corner, sounding like a deaf person trying to say something.

My face burned red and neck sore. I thought, please, please let out your grief, let's not go through this again.

I stopped contrasting Pa and Dan, beginning to compare the two, having more in common than differences. I understood Dan for trying to strangle me, violating his space but now he took his frustration out on me. For a short period, I told myself the onslaught was understandable as the man lost his wife. No! What happened was the same irrational alcohol induced bullshit Pa dished out on a regular basis. I didn't want to accept they could be two manifestations of the same creature, pointless because that was heartbreaking. I was an object of their aggression, this banded them and not something I could not let go.

Dan sobbed, not wanting to look but I did have feelings watching him breakdown. Cognitive empathy is not something one can control. It just happens, like warm champagne frothing. It is a gene therefore built-in, one day you'll be running from a bomb and turn back to pick up a child. It's who we are!

Was it the shock of the accident? There was something of the man I preferred, appearing sober. Perhaps it was the huge release of adrenalin as the pickup spun, or all the other stuff injected into his brain, as he slapped me, which eased the effects of alcohol. The hit in the balls and crying like a baby didn't go amiss. His eyes cleared, back from 'that place', surprising me.

"Things can get a little out of hand."

Finding that a really mean pun.

"Okay," Dan said, eyeing me suspiciously before what sounded like a reluctant and muffled sorry.

What was he sorry for, the accident, the beating, the crying? I wasn't going to say, 'It's Okay, apology accepted.' I wanted to move on, getting out, walking over to the driver's side.

There was significant damage, explaining the loud crash, the last four feet on the right-side smashed in. I wasn't going to tell him.

Dan continued to whimper and must have muttered the word sorry, a dozen times in three miles. It was the only time I ever heard him say it, managing to prove how worthless the word is. Sorry can mean everything or nothing. I've said it a thousand times begging not to be struck when I had nothing to be sorry about. The word is useless without clarification. There are different kinds of sorry, the tones differentiate from the sincere, to those who reel it off as a remedy for repeated bad behavior. There are those who become good actors mixing it with faux emotion, also known as a lie. Then there's the blank face sorry, the lethal version said by a serial killer in a monotone voice coupled with an emotionless face. Inevitably a knife starts hacking at your throat. In Dan's case it's the stupid 'because I'm drunk' sorry. The most meaningless of them all.

The church parking lot was full, scores of folks congregating at the entrance. I ditched the pickup, taking Dan in via the kitchen, through the side hall delivering him to the Pastor.

Dan appeared collected the whole way, gait roughly consistent, back straight. He looked scared, not knowing what he will see, yet mesmerized by the inevitable outcome. The coffin will be there. Martha will lie inside.

Dan breathed deeply, obligatorily shaking the Pastor's hand.

A visible jolt of energy swelled as he turned surveying the sight. Martha lay in a pine casket before a mass of people, every pew full, some stood to the side, others in the back. The spectacle an indication of the communities' respect for Martha. They weren't gawkers.

Dan held the Pastors' hand soaking in his life, shoulder's softened and his true realization of Martha's death came to life. At that moment Dan was human, vulnerable, emotion for everyone to see, feel. I looked away.

The Pastor motioned Dan to his wife's coffin, kneeling before it, opening his eyes wide, taking in one last image before slamming them shut. He held dignity to a point, and then slouched, weeping, the Pastor eventually sending me to take Dan to his seat. The crowd pushed their shoulders back and held their breath for a second. Eyes were fixated on me and not Dan. Why did I get stuck with this role?

The Pastor began his condolences, blessings, and prayers. Martha's eulogy was delivered by the Pastor who spoke of her good life, one based on honor and respect.

Martha's father was the Mayor at some point. He talked of Mayor Brown's achievements and how his daughter followed in his footsteps being active in the community running to those who needed help. He said, "She was a cornerstone to all of us."

111

I figured Martha was a local girl but not realizing the farm originally belonged to Martha's family, assuming it was from Dan's lineage. There was a photo in the living room of Martha standing next to two boys, one younger and one older. I imagined they were her brothers. Where was the younger, perhaps making his own life, moving away knowing he wouldn't get the farm? That doesn't explain why didn't the elder brother didn't get the farm?

I found it a coincidence that Martha's maiden name was the same used in the law suit I read in the paper, the land dispute, wondering if they were the party mentioned, remembering the legal bills and was convinced. Death is final but always opens up another chapter.

The procession to the graveyard was solemn, the younger skipping offering contrasting joy. Folks were both somber and inquisitive. When their eyes weren't on the ground looking sad, they were on me. One man chuckled, forgetting my face was beaten, and suddenly burning red, not only from embarrassment, but from throbbing pain which I had ignored.

There was one pair of particularly impertinent ladies I assumed were related to Martha, being a variance of the lady herself, hating the way they ever so quietly, oohed and aahed.

Martha was laid to her resting place, Pastor beginning a final prayer. It was a dreamy, misty, inescapable place to be. I was part of the scene, yet should have been nothing more than a spectator. I became an onlooker at myself, and then from above, floating backwards, my vision marred by clouds. I hated it.

The sun radiated, dark clothes absorbing heat, collar irritating my sweaty neck. The Pastor's wife handed Dan a posy to throw on his wife's coffin, his face tightening realizing it was over.

Dan looked back, uneasy, realizing his vulnerability thought this an intrusion and I shouldn't see him like this. The Pastor distracted him coming to shake his hand. The man of God did his job choosing to support his parishioner, clasping his hands with both palms. The touch was gentle at first but grew stronger, filling Dan with hope. He was on the brink of breakdown before a gaggle of women came with a cocktail of condolences and cutting words.

"She was a good woman. God help her soul," one plump, pious person said.

"Heart to weak for a man like that," another harped.

One old lady, black from head to toe, said. "It should never have been."

Confused I swung my head, Dan's face quickly against mine, wishing I didn't remind him to clean his teeth.

"Don't hang so close boy. Wait for me."

***

I leant against the pickup, feeling giddy, sweat pouring down my face. God, why was I so confused? All those people looking at me, not knowing which version they saw. All their imaginations sparking like fireworks on the 4th of July watching me walk Dan to his seat.

Frustrated I ripped off my tie tossing it with my jacket in the back seat. I would have rested in the front, but the windshield acted like a magnifying glass melting the faux leather. There was one place, a nearby tree offering shade, a respite from the burning sun and the whole event.

Emotionally tired I slumped on the grass, it seemed cool, starting to 'shut down', a defense mechanism against mayhem, closing my eyes, easing my muscles while working my spine from buttock to neck on the bark.

The muscles in my eyes relaxed, enjoying the reprieve from endless signals bombarding my brain like missiles, a sense of peace, relief from an angel. My thoughts were none purposely blocking all sound, but it got louder.

"Hey, John," hearing him say my name time and time again. He annoyed me from the start, eyes remaining closed wanting to enjoy every last second.

It was Simon, what did he want? This was not a good time, a very bad time, fearing my reaction.

113

"How's it going?" Simon's face was always cheery, loving him for that until eternity. His naïve bliss not able to read my expression, angry, confused, frustrated… Stay away!

"Could be better." I only answered because I liked him.

"Sorry about Martha."

"I didn't know the women."

This wasn't an invitation for Simon to tell all he knew. Intelligence, knowledge, call it what you like, these are Simon's best assets. Use them wisely!

"She was from around here. Those folks talking to Dan must be some kind of cousins," he mused.

"You know this or making this shit up," not entirely convinced, knowing Simon swung from stuff he'd learned to the occasional youthful hypothesis.

"I know…asked," defending himself. Simon only mounted verbal defenses and I knew that, making this all the more terrible.

"Asked who?"

Breaking down this barrier of knowledge and logic was going to easy, pushed on by anger for nothing, for no one, for the unknown.

"Mr. Stenton."

Simon is an honest man making my relentless questions all the more despicable. I wanted him to push me, knowing in my evil heart, his pacifist philosophy prevented him from retaliation.

"You're fucking lying. Stenton left right after service."

My mind rose above my body, circling my prey, thinking I was an eagle flying above. In fact, I was nothing but a lame vulture choosing a no contest situation. The hate for myself, for everything, fueling me.

"No a few days ago." Simon not happy with where this was going.

"What you doin' talking to Mr. Stenton about Martha?" For an instant seeing Simon as having no real feelings. It's a problem of mine, the swing from feeling everything to sometimes feeling nothing. If I took a swipe at him, it wouldn't matter.

"As I said! I asked," Simon immediately looking down.

I knew a mis-truth when I saw one. "You're a nosy little bastard." I snapped.

"When Martha died, there was talk."

"Which you over-heard?'

Simon didn't deny it. My body wanted a victim, brain switched over, hovering, considered my options.

"They were talking… well…like history."

I, like any animal before the final attack, reviews everything. Simon might have more information, fluttering in an upward wind surveying the landscape in 360 degrees.

"Sounds all too educated for a simple Simon," throwing an emotional explosive.

Simon's face turned red. Furious his voice went up a couple of octaves spitefully saying, "I know lots… I do."

"What the fuck you know then. Still haven't told me anything I don't *already* know?"

"I know Martha's had two brothers."

"Know that."

"The older one died, the younger one lives in Atlanta, some big shot business guy or something."

"I figured."

Not giving Simon any satisfaction directly acknowledging this was new. "How did he die then, Mr. Historian?"

Simon's answer is why sarcasm is never a good idea.

"Dan killed him."

There are moments when silence has a whole new meaning, like the moment you realize the drug actually works. I couldn't keep it like that forever, hearing what he said, reality setting in, evil rising, wanting to seize on the moment when Simon would say some crap giving me final justification.

"You want me to piss in your mouth, wash all the crap out?" A jealous based statement, knowing nothing while Simon knew everything.

115

"It was an accident." Simon said quietly, trying to pacify me, aware of the scrutiny in my face.

Gliding on warm winds, the prey was showing me where others lived, waiting until the time was right.

"Dan killed him by accident?" Simon repeated.

This meant nothing to me.

"Yeah, they went hunting, his gun went off, or something like that."

Simon being detailed orientated realized the ending, 'or something like that' was a mistake making a reactionary move, backing away.

My animal was almost dead, no place to go.

"...or something like that!" I was pissed. Simon's comments were idle gossip.

He tried to mount a defense, clarifying, "... no one would really know if it was an accident, now would they? ... only Dan's word for it. Think about it."

Simon appeared satisfied in his conclusion and to some extent I was, but wasn't ready for anymore 'truths'. The possibility of Dan taking his brother-in-law into the woods to blow his brains out became all too real. I wasn't prepared for this, observing from high above watching Simon scurry from shit hole to shit hole.

Simon was a much nicer guy when he shared what he learned and not playing the speculation game. Unfortunately Simon's speculation fitted the crime with the accused. It all could easily be true. The very real possibility that I lived with a very dark person made my skin flush, invisible razors peeling layers of skin. I'm about to shoot the messenger, beginning my final decent, eyes peeled on his pulsating Adam's apple, snatching Simon's scrawny throat, tightening my grip.

"Who are you to ask questions? Who the fuck are you anyway?" Throwing him to the ground.

"I'm... just...saying...like." Simon gasping.

This pissed me off even more, "Just supposing what? Mr. Adams killed him on purpose, just supposing uh!"

116

I hated the premise because knew in my heart it was true, terrifying, scaring me. Still someone must pay, tempted to take off my belt wanting to hear him scream as the buckle punctured his pink skin.

Pain is noise at first, but after a while it's like music with dips, crescendos and melodies as those suffering spew their symphony. The images became too alive to control, my foot firmly on Simon's head, whipping off my belt, doubling it, taking practice swings into my palm.

Simon regained his breath and with remarkable control, defiantly said, "Your torturing your own soul not mine."

I hesitated, out the corner of my eye a group of men ran towards us. The blood in my veins turned from boiling hot to icy cold. Being caught fighting was never a good thing.

Simon started to get up, putting my belt back on, all men talking at once.

"You Okay." One man said concerned with Simon's well-being while two pointed fiercely at me. "This is a funeral" and "You'd better have a darn good meaning for this boy," they snarled.

"He was spreading lies and gossip," pointing at my victim.

All the men looked at Simon accusingly.

"I did not," objecting and believable. "Only came to see if he was okay."

The men realized my story unlikely, Dan walking quickly towards us. His stride definitive, arms swaying, looking straight at me. With a swift hand he had me by the collar marching me to the truck.

"You, I will deal with later and don't cause any more fucking trouble."

"I was defending you."

"Me?" Astonished. "I can defend myself. That's you're fucking problem you're always trying …"

I was pleased Dan broke off, flushed, eyes growing darker, brow knotted, crazy breaking through his forehead.

Less than five minutes he was back, slamming the car door and speeding back to the farm. I feared Dan would spin off into a mental tangent, but there was nothing I could do about it. It would be like the sun setting, inevitable. He thrashed me once today, after all.

I checked reality and re-counted my behavior. At Martha's funeral I let out my feelings on Simon, someone who's doctrine doesn't even allow for retaliation. To make things worse he only stayed back to check on me, if only I had known, feeling like diarrhea from Hitler's ass-hole. Why Simon? There wasn't anyone else and I didn't know any different.

Dan concentrated on the wheel, gripping tightly, focusing on the road. He was where he should be, with priorities. The image of his dead wife fading, overridden by the chaos created when hearing an apparent truth.

When we got home, Dan drank, and I thought for an instant it would be nice to know why. The answer lied in Korea and almost definitely in his childhood, what happened? Approaching the man wasn't possible. At our most buddy moments, in the early weeks, checking each other out I asked, receiving a severe negative reaction. It was like I put a rattlesnake down his back. Now I know why, my questions pushed the PTSD button. Something once created exists forever, never disappearing like nuclear waste, and deadly like the bomb itself. Living with a person sitting next to a little red button is scary, especially since Dan hadn't 'dealt with me' so far.

***

The morning began with Dan being moody. I said little, did everything, and that is how I made it through the day, clear Dan should have nothing to complain about. This was my strategy, defense of course. Criticism could lead to anywhere, one well practiced having an alcohol ridden father.

That evening, my problem continued, not knowing who was in the hump-backed chair. Pa and Dan twitching back and forth, blurring my mind. This was happening every day.

There was the emblematic glass of amber liquid, profile partially illuminated by the lamp, arms flat on each side of the chair, hands gripping the corners.

Dan picked, "Where's my paper boy? Not going to have to tell you again."

I didn't respond instantly.

Dan grimaced before barking. "Get my paper."

It was enough, my day beginning hours before Dan even opened an eyelid. He wanted coffee when he woke up and I always left food. The bread he usually crumbled into millions of pieces, food he smashed before eating half. Food had become an accessory to alcohol. Start with bad habits and end up with bad people.

Initially I froze before running down the lane, breeze feeling good, the sprint releasing frustration. I wanted to make a joke out of my one and only mistake of the day… or try to.

Sweaty, flushed, I tossed the paper into his lap. "Wow, thanks for the workout." Gasping for breath. "It's been one hell of a day. I need a bath."

"Stop boy."

It wasn't enough for him, looking at me expectantly.

"Unwrap the paper." Dan couldn't have said it a nastier way.

Yes, I have done that before, gladly, many times in fact, but that was not now. Right now, I'm tired. Dan repeated the command leaving no compromise. My reaction time once again to short leaving him writhing. A shot of fear hit my guts, instinctively my mind de-compartmentalizing, pertinent parts of my brain running from my skull, all shouting, 'Wish I could help you buddy', being somewhat familiar with the possible road ahead.

His body language and verbiage said it was going to be best to do what he said. I knew it. My father and Dan consume the same space, almost. Dan added an extra complication being overtly sexual, like that was a part of it, later wondering if my father's antics contained a secret sexual element deciding not. I think the only reason mother stayed with him, was because he never asked for sex. He was obtusely unsexual, never hearing him make a dirty joke, always shy of his body, and would probably have a heart attack if

I shouted 'vagina' time and time again. The child he had was an accident that I knew, might not be so good at reading and writing but can correlate dates.

The paper lay on his lap, completing the task as he desired, would mean touching close to his groin. His eyes were planted on mine; goading me wanting me to reach and grab the paper next to his expanding, white-cotton shorts.

I took the paper very gently, at which point he looked at his groin, flicking his dick under his shorts. I returned the paper, unwrapped, Dan snatching it out of my hand.

"Maybe you should start remembering to get my paper, boy," snarling.

"I did what you asked. Sorry I will not forget again."

My soul knew my apology, in his mind, was pathetic and insufficient, wanting to avoid his anger turning to get away. Dan lunged forward, grabbed the back of my pants, pulling me down onto him. Confused I tried to get up, his grip tightening on my waist band and underwear, whacking my back.

"Stop!" I shouted, not willing to take a beating even with a newspaper.

Dan made cheetahs look slow, out of the chair, pushing my head to the floor, using the paper on my butt, swipes beginning to hurt.

"If you feel the fucking paper you might not forget it." He stopped, grabbed the top of my pants and with one forceful rip exposed my butt. Dan discarded the paper, sandpaper palms whacking my ass cheeks, each stung, hurting me.

"I think you want to feel something else." He was quiet for a minute, knowing the words would slowly sink and the dozen innuendos would leave me wondering and petrified.

Was Dan being experimental? Didn't know, scared wondering how deep, dark and fiery today's hell is going to be. He made it a ritual, parading around me taking swipes, chuckling when they stung, like a juvenile celebrating a big score in an arcade game.

I didn't know what was going on, Dan did, grabbing my head, pushing it towards his groin, smothering my face, holding it there making me smell man.

"I know you want this, couldn't stop looking since the day ya got here," He smiled saying it, like he was waiting all this time. "Okay, you little fuck! I sucked your cock now you're gonna suck mine and do it right this time."

I did try, moreover thought about it. We lay on a bed with fresh sheets, bodies straight out the shower and gently I would service him, but he grabbed my hair and held my jaw open, looking me in the eye, lips puckering, spit landing in my mouth.

"I want to cum hard this time. Ya hear me boy."

Dan tugged to expose himself, white rod poking out his shorts.

"Don't say you don't like it."

I hesitated, a second too long, a slap crossed my cheek.

"Do as you're told boy. I ain't messin', saw you and Stenton's boy."

My jaw almost unhinged Dan inserted his cock into my mouth. There was no time to get used to it, head already at the back of my throat, shaft pumping, oxygen supply a problem, deeper and deeper wanting to be sick.

"Urgghhh," a slew of thick saliva dribbled down my chin and over his balls. I couldn't breathe, suddenly he pulled away.

"Start working it boy."

Taking the head, massaging with my hands.

"No boy, you got to suck, just like I sucked you."

Down came another slap, harder, it stung, my cheeks flushed. Dan seeking a type of satisfaction I could never give, nor want to. I didn't want him to hurt me. These were my first realizations Dan liked it this way, having no choice, grabbing his shaft plunging my mouth onto him.

"Good boy." Dan seemed pleased. "If you play with that Simon boy, you can play with me."

There were few seconds that day when his voice, loud as it was, didn't appear to come closer. I thought it was my mind playing tricks concentrating on Simon, but now I know why. It was shocking, not that he caught us, more how devious he could be even when his heart was supposedly struck with the worse possible grief.

Not entirely satisfied Dan grabbed my hair thrusting his length wanting to fuck my gullet, pushing back before a mix of puke and saliva hit the floor.

"Lick 'em boy," pushing my head under his musty, sweaty balls. Frantically I licked, tongue touching the soft leathery texture of his scrotum, pubic hair tickling my face. I could have done this on a bro basis. We'd be experimenting, and I'd find it fascinating the way his mushroom head felt against my lips, the taste of salty precum, but Dan wanted forceful sex where the other doesn't participate.

"Get off your knees, sit down." Dan commanded, taking a fist full of hair, twisting it like a psychopathic hairstylist, scalp lifting from my skull. Following his direction was the only option, sitting on my butt, his legs above my shoulders, solid sets of quadriceps keeping me in place.

The way he put his cock in my mouth wasn't only sexual but also sinister, his mind playing with ideas. I said it before, this was an expanding ritual leading to hell for me or someone else. Watching me almost suffocate turned him on. He didn't want it soft, slow and loving, wanting an object, a living doll he could toss around.

I wanted it to be over, yet another assault and he was hurting me. My cheeks stung, jaw hurt and wanted to vomit. My clothes and floor were covered with saliva, his balls and thighs sticky.

I fondled his oversized testicles, trying to excite him hoping he would orgasm faster and leave me alone, sucking and jerking his cock, my other hand massaging the base while my mouth bounced on the rest. I thought this would please him, initially he groaned, but looked down and took another swipe at my face.

"Na, na don't touch my cock…mouth only."

As Dan thrusted, I moved not wanting it so deep, his balls tightened, glands swelled.

"Fuck yeah boy, don't stop…don't you dare fucking stop." His grip on my skull intensified. "Oh yeah boy, eat it, boy."

Dan's penis pulsated, almost bouncing in my mouth, body shuddering. He wasn't a screamer, that telling me a lot, that he was used to being quiet when letting go, like he didn't want anyone to hear him. A man who makes loves to his wife doesn't care about that.

There was a new taste in my mouth, a little at first then a gush, sweat, slightly fishy but also meaty, followed by an acrid taste that I disliked. He pumped again, spurts hitting deeper into my throat.

"Hold out your tongue boy," was one of the last commands, squeezing out last drops, clamping my jaws shut. His breath eased, nasty smile dissipating.

"Oh Fuck." Dan looked down, my cheeks scarlet, pants ripped, hair pulled, saliva and bits of puke on the floor, trying to gather myself. There was no way he was going to get away with this. No eye to eye contact made that clear.

"You bastard," turning to retreat. "I ain't cleaning up that mess."

Dan was silent and didn't move, cock still hanging out his underwear. He looked very stupid.

The taste of his semen was horrible, burning deep in my throat, probably from all the whiskey, making it to the bathroom before wrenching into the toilet. I swilled and spat but the taste remained.

The night seemed endless, made no sense. If he was loving, I would have sucked his dick, happily. Dan was charismatic, could be charming even captivating. Why couldn't he ask me to join him on the couch? Encourage a man to man massage, guiding me, slowly letting me know where he needs attention. I would have done it, my chance to take control, hands and mouth defining how long it would take, stopping to look into those emerald eyes, defiantly stating everything was up to me. In an ideal world I'd like to fasten his ankles and wrists, so he couldn't fight my teasing tongue. Once he couldn't take anymore, myself prepared for an hour, I'd make sure it felt good, not that much of an asshole, but the skull-fucking left me hating him.

Hate like never before and I'm no stranger to hate. It's not like I am hateful. Hate comes to you, it's disgusting, revolting and that's why we hate it. I didn't choose to be Dan's toy. It was time to leave, get out! How? He paid only at the end of the season. My wallet contained $2.68 cents.

Remembering my original feelings, he seemed easy, friendly and unconcerned. Joviality and patience bought trust which decayed after the pondside experience. Dan was pissed I didn't suck him like he wanted, despite me trying to be a good buddy. Now all of this because he was leaking, and in his addled mind thought I owed him a blow job. More problematic was his impending jealousy of Simon.

Sleep was illusive. The same thoughts circling, spiraling in a sphere like living inside a

ping-pong ball. If he wasn't fully charged, what else would he have done? - was one of the thoughts incarcerating me in this small space, mind unable to break free.

I determined Dan had gotten used to a bend-over-boy, imagining him lugging the victim to the old barn, sometimes squealing, sometimes not. The old stained mattress gave a lot away. But that was part of the problem, I was a squealer, and combined with Martha death, Dan's life and focus was skewed.

Forgiving him was not something I was going to do. My curiosity in the same sex disappeared. For the next week, I went to my room filling my imagination with one female figure after the other. Despite their boxy faces I fucked Mary Beth and Mary Ann doing some darn right, bad-assed shit, and one evening Mr. Stenton's wife was my mummy, defiantly groaning before climax, hoping he heard everything and saw the mess. He wouldn't, I'm the fuck-head who does the laundry. Maybe I shouldn't change my sheets, stain the whole lot and wait for the smell to permeate.

***

Dan was being remarkably civil. He was getting up when he should, washed twice a day, ate his food, worked a normal day, and drank a lot less. Still I wasn't speaking to him.

I was trying to make food and fucking it up when he came to help. He didn't criticize, calmly sorted it out and within ten minutes we ate. The following nights he continued to help with dinner, getting frustrated with my silence and stony aura.

He hadn't said sorry or anything about the event. The ball wasn't on my side of the court and from my point of view didn't want him to hit it back. Game over buddy.

Dan asked if I wanted a beer. He worked me hard that day and nothing seemed better. Are we back to two guys hanging in their shorts, Dan scratching every ten minutes? I don't think so! But the alcohol did soften my mood. I guess it was his way to start an apology.

"You wanna go to that dance?" Pausing, "Take that Simon boy."

"Dance?" Suddenly confused.

"Yeah, you know, the Summer Harvest Fest…" pausing to eye me, "Don't pay much attention at church, do you?"

I pondered; my preliminary thought is obvious, pussy, then considered this an opportunity to run.

"Sounds great. You're not going?"

"Been more than thirty times." Dan finally revealing something about himself.

"You from Caravelle?"

"Yes, sure you know that."

"No, I know nothing about you, every time I ask something you say something else. Who's your father?

"A farmer, a fucking farmer, who you think?" Irritation rising, not wanting to anger him, but he checked himself.

"Sorry of course." Again I apologized for nothing, it was a reasonable question, he could have expanded and told me he had a great Dad, took him fishing, except I thought that wasn't true.

"Hey, buddy." Holding up arms defensively, his shell cracking "Oh God... it's just been so," reaching for his brow. I thought of pending repentance which never came, instead he collected himself before muttering, "I didn't mean that, or anything."

The night he bitched me up I initially put his behavior down to the loss of his wife, money problems, and frustration before dispelling these as excuses. He didn't deserve excuses, just a simple bastard, Dad plus one. In the interim, however, he had changed his ways, doing what he should, acting like a human. He confused me, perhaps the 'good Dan' winning a few battles for once.

"Yeah. I get it."

Did I really? Dan was a man spreader, staring at it. He stared at me and then downwards.

It's been a week since I came down my throat. I wash his sheets, nothing, underwear only stained with urine and shit and he wasn't jerking off in the woods or the bathroom. Dan wasn't the kind of guy who jerks off, period. It certainly wasn't leaking out his ears, like so many wish it would.

Was this my opportunity to do it my way? No! it was clear he liked like it rough and after the second night he'd became interactive making a play for my ass. It'll be like putting a tiger and a fawn in the same cage. A fair analogy considering I have nowhere to run.

If I said no, however, he might demand it, simply pushing me to my knees in a repeat session of seven days past. Dan worked his bulge, the same wet patches appearing on his cotton shorts.

"Thanks for the beer, been a long day," stretching and yawning to accentuate my tiredness.

Dan was quick to respond, "Are you sure son?" Reaffirming what was on display.

I saw the comment as a threat. "Yes, I am very sure."

This was the first time I looked Dan in the eye since I gargled his ejaculate. That wasn't going to happen again, making the conscious decision to fight, storming up the stairs. "Buy yourself a fucking Playboy."

***

Dan wasn't happy all day long, perhaps blue balls governing his mind, don't know nor care. It wasn't my problem. I slaved, not a thing to say, making him keep his promise snatching the keys before he could relinquish. The pickup was full of gas, that was something.

The feeling of freedom took over, accelerating to top speed. I didn't care if there was someone traveling in the opposite direction, either I was gonna get pussy or not.

Simon was going to be my wingman, the guy that made me look good. This was going to be a great night.

"You ready buddy?"

"Darn right I am."

He clambered in, exuberant as I, impossible to talk, my mind filled with the smells and tastes of women.

Simon looked more than squeaky clean, apparently even had some aftershave, but the scent was slightly sweet reminding me more of a perfume. It suited him.

Summer Festival

The band played on a stage almost the size of a basketball court, lights flashing from above, behind, mixes of colors only seen in my dreams. A spotlight focused on the singer, who was the cutest thing I've seen to date, petite with lioness lungs, louder than anything I've heard.

A packed crowd two-stepped before the music picked up into a swing, followed by a raucous square dance. Guys stamped their feet hard, as if performing a mating ritual. They were!

Simon and I stood on the sidelines having asked every spare chick in the place to dance. They either squirmed like worms sensing light or 'are you serious?'

"Hey Si, lets walk around a bit. There's nothing here."

He couldn't hear me, the music blasting but still he followed.

Despite the apparent joy, a night filled with bright lights from the Ferris wheel and shrieks from the roller coaster, I felt alone, all the noise disappearing for an instant. So many people and no female companion to talk to, dance with, kiss, only for one night. This is not what I was imagining.

"Si, let's have a beer, you're paying."

The vendor insisted, not without an adult. I wasn't of age.

There was a woman looking at me, sipping her drink slowly, short little sips, puckering her lips on the straw. I couldn't ignore her stare, it was intense, and she wasn't going to stop.

"That's my Aunt," handing over the money, casually strolling towards Simon. I didn't walk quickly, fruitless to show her I'm a baby running from Mama. Anyway, escaping this woman's gaze was impossible, her eyes peeled. I straightened my back, flexed, mostly to cool my nerve, sauntering, intrigued. She needed to know I noticed her, looking back giving her firm acknowledgment. Her beady, provocative eyes responded.

"Looks like you boys came out for some fun." The woman slowly walking towards us, drink held high to her mouth, still taking short sips, stopping a few feet away.

She was a mature woman, hair bleached blonde styled into a neat bob, long curls on each side accenting a heart-shaped face. Her make-up was heavy, but with a vermillion, paneled skirt, shorter than everyone else, and a crisp, white collared shirt open a little too far, she looked like a dream.

"Yeah." Loud, being authoritative, the one in charge, giving my first glance to Simon to zip it.

"Well," she said, taking another sip. "Are you having any fun?" Her eyes were brown, long, black eyelashes guarding her from the outside world looking in.

"Yeah, sure we are." I said.

Simon just shrugged his shoulders. He was being honest.

"Well you don't sound convinced," she said quietly, framing each word perfectly with scarlet lips. She left her mouth open, tongue caressing teeth as she looked me over, up and down, and then to Simon.

I felt awkward and blurted out. "We're not from here."

"Well neither am I. We have something in common, that's good." Her voice sweet, like listening to pure sugar.

"Oh really," I said.

Simon came closer, curiosity spiking. "So, what you doin' here?"

"Same as you boys, looking for a little fun," her movements sultry, "but I haven't had any yet," slurring. This pretty creature was well dressed, purse expensive and earrings sparkling like real diamonds.

"Doesn't seem to be a good place for a lady. What's your name?" Standing closer than Simon, a primal move showing I was going to protect her, and she should ignore the scrawny dude next to me.

She lit a cigarette, chuckling, amused. "My name is...," tossing her head to the side considering what to say, "...Ruby," bursting into laughter.

129

She took a long pull blowing smoke in my face. She was drunk. Women in this state, in public spaces, are something I have watched out for in a past life, almost always offering an opportunity, but at the time I didn't know what to make of her. She must be someone's wife judging by the wedding ring.

"So." Not focusing. "What do you boys call yourselves?"

Simultaneously we said our names. Simon blushing held out his hand, "Nice to meet you Maam."

Ruby didn't take it, disgusted at his limp wrist.

"I was hoping you boys could do me a favor," still slurring, suddenly serious, keeping the same slow speech, lips dancing, annunciating every word.

Simon, quiet, let me speak, "Of course, anything we can do."

"I need someone to drive me home…," pausing for eternity, body shimmering, "… the roads are dark."

My thoughts were darker than any road and I'd give her protection, my special protection, millions of my babies swimming inside her.

A smile lit up on Simon's face, shutting him off, knowing it was a mistake to sound eager. "We'd be happy to oblige," not sure of this lady's intention but hoped it was similar to mine.

"You seem like nice boys. I can trust you," confident, monotone, adding an edge of seriousness and possible consequence. Ruby made us trustworthy.

"Of course, you can." Simon blurting out, nudging him in the side. That's superfluous.

"I have my own car. All I need is a driver." It was like listening to honey. "And I want you to drive," pointing at me.

Simon is a good buddy, piping up, "I'll follow on behind."

Ruby stopped in her tracks, "Maybe that's a good idea," smirking, "One of you might go bust on me. Back up is always good," laughing.

Following her to the car I replayed what she said and thought my conclusion was fair, the three of us were going to have sex. Or was it an innuendo? …except I didn't know what one was.

The vehicle was new, powder blue, the emblem recognizable as Chrysler. A Caprice was something special.

"Where we heading?" I inquired.

"Elton."

Simon was close behind and heard. "I'll meet you by the gas station," darting off. Without that tip, I would have looked like a fool asking for direction.

I sat next to a beautiful lady. Occasional glances meant she might like to chat.

"May I ask your name Maam, your real name?"

"Why?"

Every movement planned and perfectly timed, like a mini Broadway show.

"Because Ruby is a name which…" Shit, gulping, recovering. "The name of a lady who might work in a bar," committed, "and I don't think you work in a bar."

"Maybe that's why I like the name. It's how I want to feel."

"Guess you're right. I ain't never going to forget you," sighing, "So it won't make a darn bit of difference." The sentiment charmed her.

We turned our heads at the same time, straightening my body, flexing, toned from the summer's work. She saw my bulge, signifying approval, relaxing, her legs further apart, skirt riding up her thighs. My pants were tight and not because I wore 'the fashionable pair', more my thighs and butt had developed and now too small.

 I snuck another look. Her hand starting to caress the inside of her leg.

I shouldn't have said anything but did, "Wow, I really will never forget you."

She smiled, cheekily, fingers working themselves towards her crotch.

The worst thing is to think about comes next! In the world of novice, it can even kill a boner. Overall a bad thought process, but truly wanted to stop the car and do it by the side

131

of the road, not caring about the shocked faces of parents and children as they drove home from the Summer Festival.

It has to be instinctual, taking my foot off the gas, lowering the gear, slipping my hand on her knee. Her legs naturally opened, silk stockings showing her shape topped with scarlet lace, panties barely covering a plump womanhood.

My fingers, rough against her stocking, traveled upwards feeling soft flesh, heating up an already sticky and balmy night. There was no space left in my pants, taking a deep breath, like the gasp before an orgasm, except it hurt.

I couldn't be distracted. More importantly was how far I could take this lady. If I played my cards right my time will come, hopefully, literally.

We reached the top of a hill, lights of a small town twinkling in the distance. My touch was gentle at first, but she seemed eager, maybe at the prospect of approaching our destination, legs opening as far as the seating allowed. I pulled her flimsy panties aside, fondled her bush, tickling her clitoris, feeling her heat. My fingers quickly became moist touching her opening, a little deeper, she tightened, examining her intricate muscle structure.

My fingers are fat. Maybe this was more than a finger fuck, possibly a little dick fuck, don't know, but she groaned. The walls of her vagina were slippery and closing in, swinging her hand to grab my crotch while letting out a vocal and physical gush of pleasure. Fluid squittered around my fingers, mind lost, my cock at the point of bursting as she rubbed me.

I probed, discovered, fantasied, even closed my eyes, and wasn't done but horns blasted, Simon flashing his lights. We'd slowed to 20mph, the trail of traffic long, smearing the gear stick I revved up.

It was difficult to concentrate, working out ways to make certain this lady was going to be very happy meeting me. I'd take her to the edge, time and time again, before throwing her off the cliff of endless ecstasy, orgasms so strong she'd have no idea if she's fully alive or about to die.

"Left at the gas station, turn into Blanchette Road," eyes shut, hair astray, struggling to organize her underclothes.

The road winded up and out the valley. There was a sign, nicely made, Blanchette Road, but there was no, 'next' or a specific 'Blanchette Road'. I was confused.

Woods surrounded us, the road getting better as it neared the top of the hill. The trees disappeared changing to rolling fields on the left, and to the right stone walls which only increased in size, lights sparkling in the valley below.

Someone had taken great care to create a formal entrance with walls finishing in two pillars, supporting wrought iron gates before a manicured landscape. Blanchette Road was a place, an estate with out-buildings, horse barns, and training areas, staked out with white picket fences, and not a dumpy street.

I drove cautiously, past the guardhouse to a large, colonial, brick three-story home with balconies, porticos, cornices, and other faux-French touches making the building look like a giant wedding cake, slowing the car to a crawl. There was silence except for Simon catching up, engine rumbling.

Now was the time to make my move but couldn't say what I was thinking. Ma did raise a gentleman after all. "You need me to help you inside."

Ruby had become someone else, hair orderly, dress normal, attitude different.

She gave a sly grin, "No," then a faint smile, confidence replaced with vulnerability and fear, desperately leaning over to kiss her.

"You sure you don't wanna be Ruby a bit more," throwing my weight towards her, hand instantly making a move towards the prize.

"Ruby has gone home honey, and so should you," shoving me off.

I got the message, but that does mean I have to like it, feeling like a soldier in the desert who thought he saw an oasis. Ruby was very nervous. I didn't know why, she didn't know why, then it became clear.

There was a loud click, the encompassing noise of a powerful electrical circuit beginning. Lights flooded from bushes and down from all corners of the mansion, exposing the estate, exposing us.

"Go, he'll kill you." She commanded, fear evident in her face. The pretty mother with a slutty side now a scared child. "He's not supposed to be here," she screamed, "Get out."

Simon was a hundred feet away. I jumped out rocketing towards the pickup, waiving to Simon, men's voices behind me.

"Who the fuck is that?" A man shouted. "Was he kissing you." I heard a whack.

Ruby cried, begged, and then the firecracker sound of a gun. Simon realized we had a problem, was back in the car and turning it around. A bear at full speed is fast, I was no exception tilting my body forward for full acceleration before straightening to a full bolt. Bullets flew past, hitting the back end of the truck, only feet to go. Simon had the passenger door open, diving into the moving vehicle. The man was not giving up, blasting a couple of 'fuck you' rounds, bullets striking the rear and side of the pickup as we swerved down the driveway.

Simon raced, after those gates we were out of it. A light went on in the gatehouse, a window on the second floor opened. We were less than thirty feet away with a man staring down the barrel of a shotgun. This was a good thing, since he didn't have time to shut the gates, but a bad thing as his chances of killing us were high.

"Down," I shouted.

He fired the first blast, metal hit metal, the windshield cracked, pickup swerved. The second blast exploded the windshield into a million shards flying like diamonds in the night sky. I snatched the wheel, blind guessed which direction, the vehicle skidding out the gates and bolting down the hill.

I looked back, no one was following us, holding my breath. The floodlit gateway and estate disappeared, entering the woods, canopy adding an imaginary layer of security.

"Simon don't stop."

He looked at me, jaw hung, face redder than ever.

"They could still be after us. Jesus look at this car."

We briefly surveyed the damage; mirrors, windshield and rear window shot out, hood and side impregnated with lead.

On the other side of Caravelle Simon asked. "What happened back there?"

"Ruby acted all sexy. So, fucking certain I was gonna get some," wincing.

"Why were you driving so slowly? There were ten cars behind you."

"Warming her up." I tried to stretch.

Simon smiled, bashfully, knowing he wanted detail, but I wasn't going to volunteer. What happened back there was a disaster and far from happy, wanting to smash my head against a tree. Why is pussy so goddam illusive?

Simon flicked pieces of broken glass onto the road, seeing them as the last bits of my life being discarded, reacting.

"Don't do that." I snapped, "You're leaving a god damn trail."

"We already are," he mused.

The radiator was leaking.

What could be done with the pickup? - Dan recently had the blessed thing repaired! There were no good solutions. Hide it, until I broke the news to Dan was one, then it occurred to me, I've worked all summer for nothing. The little I'd be paid would go to repairing the truck, and it probably wasn't going to be enough. We were coming up to Benton.

"I wanna get rid get of this glass and take a piss," I said, Simon veering to the left. "No, in a quiet spot," irritated. "Don't go through Benton, don't want anyone seeing us. Go via Thomson's farm, we'll join the road on the other side."

The pickup was a mess spending half an hour picking out glass. I could do more, forcing me away, pulling out my cock stiff from remaining images of me fucking that women and a very full bladder. Simon was quickly by my side, too close.

"Hey man." Taking a step to the side, my urine-jet going in Simon's direction.

"Watch it," he said, starting a little stream of his own.

135

"Well don't get so fucking close," angry from what had happened. Everything was going to annoy me, because I didn't get what I wanted.

Simon only had a trickle, not really peeing, eyes traveling towards my cock. It wasn't the first time. Normally I didn't mind, even it encouraged on occasion standing in full view. This time, however, it was irritating, especially with a large wet patch in my underwear.

"What happened in the car?" Simon asked. Another attempt to find out more, shooting me a side glance, before gluing his eyes on my cock. "She, sure as hell got you going."

"I touched her. That's all you need to know."

"Left you boned up," sniggering.

Like I don't know that! If I wasn't ending my piss would have hit him there and then. Doesn't he understand the utter frustration when expectation doesn't meet reality? My bet was certain, and it didn't come through, feeling worse than the John who paid for ten minutes but needed twelve minutes to cum.

"Hey man, I'm in the same state." He retorted, pulling back his foreskin, head shiny and pink. It was almost as hard as mine, two more strokes took it the rest of the way, night bugs shrilling.

Simon's voice barely broke sound level. "I wanna be your bro."

"You are my bro," asking myself why he needed confirmation now, but he didn't mean that, surprising me, completely surprising me. Yes, I jerked him, my dick was in his mouth, almost put Simon's dick in my mouth, but when he turned slowly lowering his pants, I freaked.

"Fuck man! Get your ass out of my way," kicking hard, boot colliding with his furry ginger ass, whacking the back of his balls. He yelped like a puppy, tumbling to the dust, standing over him squeezing out more pee. He pathetically tried to fend it off, droplets landing on his face. "Get your ass back in the pickup, or I'll leave you behind."

If only he understood I wasn't expecting that, immediately wiping tears of guilt. Yet again I didn't know how to react, my insecurity causing violence.

Simon wavered, clothes and face muddy, combinations of piss and dust. Again, I destroyed this young soul, just because I couldn't communicate.

He said he wanted to be my bro and I thought about that. My curiosity had waned after Dan's version of man on man. If anything, I wanted man *with* man and here was a vulnerable creature who needs love like I need love, both coming from hate-ridden, poverty-stricken, hell holes.

He clambered in the pickup, looking more like a hobo, and it was all my fault. I didn't start the engine, Simon glancing over wondering what the problem was. His loving face vandalized by my mis-placed hatred sourced new tears. I was embarrassed, feeling guilty having done something terrible needing to be closer, putting my arm around his shoulders.

"It's okay buddy." Simon was all I had. Someone I kicked in the nuts then pissed on, feeling like scum.

Simon didn't know how to react with my bulky arm around him. I made myself say it, words Dan couldn't say when he made a mistake. I was better than him, wanted to be better than him. "I'm sorry, you took me by surprise," crying quietly, "I didn't mean to kick you."

It was Simon's faith to forgive instantly, no questions asked but he was silent. He was right, after multiple assaults, I was wasn't deserving of forgiveness yet.

Simon looked sad, empty, like he was reliving an experience? I guessed this wasn't the first time, feeling a stronger need to make it right, bringing him closer.

I said it again, wanting to, needing to, making a promise to both myself and Simon, that I am better than this creature of habit and can break this cycle. "I need your forgiveness." More apologetic tears tumbling.

Simon still didn't look me in the eyes but reacted to my hug, arms moving around my waist, lifting his head, faces inches apart. His eyes lulled in their sockets, thin pink lips open, breath on my tongue, my taste buds jumping.

137

It was here where the notion of kissing him started, wanting to seal my sorry with something he'd recognize. It's a good question to ask why, maybe I wanted to protect him, show him there was love, brotherly love.

Simon couldn't kiss me, not after spreading his butt cheeks and my reaction. His body in my arms was like a girl, slender, sweet scented and wanted nothing more in the world, letting my lips butterfly for several seconds before making it meaningful.

I wanted to keep my eyes open to see his reaction but closed them at the last minute. Initially, there was none, taking him several seconds to realize what was happening, my lips firmly on his. He couldn't believe it. The moment he'd been waiting for was here, happening now, like a meteor in the sky, after a million years of waiting.

Still Simon wasn't kissing me back.

Simon lied saying he kissed a girl. This was his first kiss absorbing the experience in silent ecstasy. He looked up to heaven like Beata Beatrix double-dosed with laudanum, past and present pain raging in the background. Whatever his experience with other men were, it didn't include kissing or any form of real love, and probably not with someone of his age. My heart bled for him, wanting to give him everything, seal him, insulate him from the world and hatred.

It took a while, his tongue flickering, coming to life, teasing the inside of my lips. I wasn't letting go, paws clasping his cheeks, controlling the intensity of our mouth swipes from tender to semi-bites.

It was like kissing a girl, having the same vulnerability. The kiss saying, 'I will protect you'. That's all we've ever wanted, protection, not only for Simon, also for me. It meant we were equal in this one sensitive way, now on a level field where affection flourishes.

Simon hands remained in a brotherly hold around my waist, understanding what happens next was up to me.

I examined options from every angle, deciding the questions my feelings bring untimely, and due to their complexity couldn't be answered now. Simon found security in my arms and we both liked it, enough.

Simon took away some of the final decision feeling delicate, kisses coming back in succession, enjoying my bristly chin. Voluntarily he stopped, opening my shirt buttons, nestling his face in my furry chest, liking the comfort moving side to side, preferring places with fur at its deepest. I hoped the tear he shed was the last of his life, Simon breathing happily. Several minutes passed, his face buried in my mane, hugging me. There wasn't much of a decision left to make, anyway, it was over. I was going to show him love exists, and exactly how it should feel.

Simon saw the bulge, my rod filling the gap between crotch and pocket. I'd have to take his hand giving him permission to touch, reaching out, fingers entwined, finally moving his hand to its destination, his eyes not leaving mine.

Giving him permission made him happy. He wanted to give love just like I did. Up to now he tried everything to show it, but I had been uneasy, unconsciously resisting with fits of fury. That is over.

Simon's face moved quickly to my groin, mouth outlining the bulge, before grappling with my zipper, having to help. Lowering my underwear, Simon waited anxiously on the moment my dribbling cock bounced out. My expression gave him all the freedom he wanted.

I was pleased he didn't suck it instead he licked me clean, tongue teasing my pee hole asking for more, taking deep breathes, enjoying my scent.

I couldn't imagine my next move; the pickup's front bench seat wasn't going to work. My beefy ass would hit the gear stick, and we'd roll down the hill.

I ran my fingers through Simon's ginger locks as he glorified his new toy, wanting adoration but not only.

There was only one way, opening the door, and before Simon could say anything he was out, body pressed against cold metal, his ill-fitting jeans falling to the ground, pulling open butt flaps engulfing tiny soft buttocks, squeezing. Simon groaned, wanting to feel him more, one hand working his butt while the other reached around. His penis was hard, wet, eagerly fucking my podgy-finger fist the same way he did before. He wasn't going to cum yet, not going to be that easy, liking the feeling of his crack especially where the skin buckled. It was sweaty, probing, Simon instinctively bending over, internal butt muscles trying to relax around my fingers.

I couldn't completely see, pressing into what I thought was butt-hole. Simon helped, pushing back his flaps then his cheeks, only a question of pushing but my cock wouldn't go in, Simon gasping at every attempt. I spat on my prize, spat on my baby maker ensuring it was going to work this time, paws grabbing his hips and pushed, Simon taking deep breaths. The tip was inside, waiting to push further. Simon didn't squeal, his mouth gaped, and eyes bulged, before making a grab for his dick poking out his piss flap.

"Oh, sweet Mary, mother of Jesus."

I pulled out, "You okay buddy?"

He didn't answer, only nodded I was doing the right thing when he felt fresh spit, my fingers probing and more spit. The circumference had widened, slowly reinserting, waiting for Simon's grimace to dissipate before burying it. The heat was intense, creating sensations I didn't know existed, enough to put me over the edge, trying to distract myself reaching around to create another of Simon's favorite, fuck-fists.

Bent over, back down, his hands grabbing tuffs of grass, wanting to feel him skin to skin, lifting his thin frame, biting his back and neck, moving in and out. The moon found space in the clouds seeing myself clearly inside him, and wanted more, withdrawing, spinning him around in a full embrace, mouth smothering his, kicking off my pants. Simon didn't quite get why this was a good idea, picking him up, planting him on the back seat. Taking off his long underwear seemed complicated, even superfluous, spreading his legs.

I didn't have to hold his buttocks or even his legs, Simon gently bouncing. Despite my pole probing him, Simon maintained an erection, surprised he wasn't touching himself. His testicles receded, barely visible, holding the base of his penis, tickling his tight scrotum comparing his genitals to mine. They were different, he was different, and I guess that was making this all possible.

Simon's stare intensified, losing control. He didn't have to masturbate, my cock massaging his prostate enough, ass muscles contracting. This time there was no way to stop what was happening, my growl getting louder. Simon was with me, an initial short spurt of semen dribbled onto his ginger bush. He grinned, feeling more pre-cum, my orgasm still mounting. Balls deep made Simon squirt harder, thicker pent-up shots artfully splattering his chest, the smell of cum filling my nostrils.

My balls were on fire, Simon's tightening sphincter acting like a cock ring. I could no more, body shuddered, convulsing, feeling it from my temples to my souls, pumping. Simon felt the shots, every one of them, grin broadening to a smile, radiant and unforgettable observing his bliss.

This was my second fuck wanting to kiss him. This is what I did to Jessie after I fucked her, but she threw me off. Simon was different reveling in the tongue taste while we remained connected. I wiped away the little tears speckling his cheeks. He did the same for me, neither of us wanting to let this go.

My first fuck with Simon was because I liked him, felt he needed love, as I did, but also because I couldn't face Dan. I have to admit that, Simon was happy, face once again buried in fur. It's where he wanted to be, feeling guilty disturbing him for the sake of my own sad reality.

I could feel the dew point, knowing it was late, eventually confessing my fear.

"I can't go back. Don't want to go back."

"You have no choice, even if you left the pickup in the lane he'll still come after you." Simon was right as usual, but I didn't want to admit it.

"Who cares?

"He cares! You are all he's got. No you, and he is…" clearly frustrated, "…nothing, gone… bankrupt."

"What if…"

 Simon broke me off. "You've forgotten who his buddy is."

"The Sherriff?"

141

"Yes. The Sherriff." Sapphire eyes saying stop.

The pickup chugged the last mile making it past the barn, parking the wreck out of direct sight. If I went to bed Dan might awake, and I'd have to tell him there and then. It was late and what would I say? Tell the truth and hear him raw with laughter, because I tangled with the rich before he beats the crap out of me.

My soul, warm from good sex was not ready for that, enjoying every love wave until there were just ripples. I replayed the event time and time again, the way Simon's body felt, the strength of my orgasm, the sincerity in his eyes during our last kiss.

At home, Jessie's brothers sought justice. Now I would have to wait for Dan's idea, and in the middle was Simon, an unlikely hero. The night wore on, the breeze cooled, my thoughts were endless, none led me anywhere. My body ached, the faux-leather soft, head slid back, and the night took over.

DAN BECOMES HIMSELF!

I was in the middle of a torrid dream sequence. The soft tapping on metal interrupted the final spiral, my car flying off a cliff, fire, trying to run but couldn't, the inferno swelled. The sound got louder, smelling his soap, opening my eyes, silhouette hiding his expression.

"Good Morning." Croaking, my throat dry.

"Had a bit of a night eh?"

"I'll make it up to you."

"You darn right you will, starting now, get to it." Dan pointed to the pasture, uncomfortable animals adding to the morning chorus.

"Yeah, sure I'll get right to it. Just gonna grab breakfast and be right there." Trying to un-collapse a body stiff from sleeping upright.

"You can get breakfast later, much later." Dan's voice was calm.

"Oh okay, gonna run inside and use the bathroom, be right back." Rapidly pacing towards the farmhouse.

"Pee in your pants for all I care. I said get to it."

His words hit me like bricks.

"No really." A fart rumbling and breaking.

Dan remained surprisingly placid. "You wanna think about how much work you're gonna do to pay for that." Pointing at the wreck.

"I'm gonna do that, gonna make it right." My shoulders were hunched, every anthropologist saying I assumed the passive position.

"Then start now," smirking.

He could see I was in pain, waste twerking in my bowel, clenching my anus as hard as I could. "You want me to dump on your courtyard?"

"No, you can shit in the field with the fucking cows." There weren't any muscles twitching in his face, voice monotone. The look meant I should surrender.

I milked the cows one painful step at a time. Dan walked past the barn door, stopping to check I wasn't crapping in the hay. When the time came, didn't mind letting it out in the field, hiding behind the herd, but soon they scattered. The humiliation sunk in, Dan standing not more than a hundred feet away. I grabbed grass while he laughed, making me feel full degradation.

I ate tomatoes, sticks of celery while working the coup cracked eggs into my mouth, and ate fruit throughout the day. Fuck him!

It was gone nine by the time I had something hot and nourishing on the table, setting the table as I did every day. Dan noticed two place settings removing mine. He took my bowl placing a small serving, looked pensive, holding back the plate, the moment petrifying me.

"You owe me something."

"Yeah I know we're going to work it out. Ma will wire money. There's my end of season money to."

"I mean you're license. You're driving license. Give me your wallet."

"No, I don't need to do that."

"Boy, you're gonna pay me back. I'm getting security. We could do this the hard way, or speak to…"

"No, stop, your buddy the Sheriff," taking the license and tossing it. The card hit the table tumbling onto the floor.

"You got your fucking license," storming off to my room, not wanting to give him time to think, as he could have easily hit me. If he was angry at my impudence, he'd need time to cool down and hopefully contemplate.

I was wrong! Dan had the next move and was playing it. There were sounds of a wood drill, a hammer, screw, and metal, knowing what he had done, trying the door. I couldn't get out.

"Hey, I need to piss." I cried.

"Should have thought about that before," amused.

"I said, I'd pay you back, I meant it."

"You boy, are what the court calls, a flight risk." Laughing finding the cliché funny.

"Fuck you! I'm gonna piss all over this fucking room."

"Boy, if you do that, I will mess you up, like you've never been messed up before. I know you Daddy beat ya, but wait until I'm through with ya."

I needed some defense, "Oh yeah, I heard about Martha's poor brother, you and him in the forest." Giving him an open ended question.

There was deathly silence, expecting a tirade, waiting for him to explode through the oak panels. Nothing, all I could hear were footsteps descending the stairs.

Hunger ran wretched, stomach contracting, gastric juices pumping with nothing to work on. I'd been hungry before, when Pa was in jail, knowing what it's like. Ma said to think about something nice and thought of Simon. Even he couldn't fight off visions of steak grilling, cutting succulent meat as juices ooze, taste finished with crispy burnt fat.

I hate being hungry, prefer pain. Pain for me, so far, was fractured bones which healed in a week or two. The mind adjusts which it can't do with hunger. You can sleep with pain but can't with hunger. I never should have stormed off, even though the amount of food he offered wouldn't have made a difference. At least the vase finally has a use.

There was too much to think about, stranded on the wiry mattress, a little raft floating in an ocean in some fucked-up horror show. I couldn't get off, couldn't get out, going crazy. I thought about violence trying to predict a winner in a physical conflict. Dan had height and experience. Our muscle was equal, I was scared, and he wasn't.

I didn't sleep that night mind wondering about ways to make a clean break. Having no money could be solvable, similar to transport. It was the threat of the Sherriff on my tail that left me scared and helpless. The Sherriff would enjoy it, knowing it. He'd make sure it wouldn't be a simple arrest but a takedown and what would happen back at the Station. His sadistic mind combined with handcuffs and a baton left me topping up my piss vase with a bit of puke. It took until dawn for reality to sink in, there was no place to go. Dan had me under control.

Dan unlocked the door fifteen minutes before I should be taking the cows in, running to the bathroom, not spilling the vase.

Dan was cold, smug and silent. He waited downstairs speaking in the same voice I heard yesterday. His sentences authoritative, devoid of emotion, coming across as 'no choice' statements.

"You have one minute to get breakfast," glancing at the clock.

This was different, normally 'breakfast' as such was after milking, checking the hens, and a bunch of daily chores. Frustrated I grappled, only taking three pieces of bread, shoving one in my mouth, and one in each pocket.

Dan kept a close eye on me, he needn't. There was nowhere to go, no options, nothing. Without an answer to money and transport, there was no escape plan.

The sun was high in the sky, Dan went in and I followed, hoping for a break. He swiveled on his heel and flicked his hand. "Don't think you have time to eat boy."

"Give me a chance to sort it out."

"I know your Ma ain't got a dime, you're lying to me, which I don't appreciate." Dan's words consistently spoken, precise, menacing.

I was embarrassed, backing off.

"I want that woodpile finished by the time I get back."

His lunch break was usually an hour but there were two hours of work.

I needed a break, it was gone noon, started just gone five. He nagged me to hurry at every opportunity, muscles ached, deciding to sit in the barn, out of sight. If there was going to be a confrontation, because I hadn't completed the work, so be it. Thirsty, the dry bread stuck in my throat staggering to the standpipe. The water revived me, letting the water flow over my neck. Then it struck me, a start, a huge start, in the old barn was a pile of junk, remembering a bicycle wheel sticking out.

The hope gave me the shot I needed. It was a seed, nothing more, enough to bring me back to work. I was good at splitting logs and made a considerable in-road before Dan returned.

He stood five yards away, staring at me. I saw no reason to stop. He did not say stop and I didn't want to talk to him. He followed my every move, feeling his eyes as I swung the ax, wondering what's the price for not finishing on time. Maybe it was ten minutes with him staring at me, hands inside pockets realizing it was fun to fuck with my head.

This was peak apple season picking bushel after bushel, dragging them to the tractor. I made one decision, meaning there wasn't unless otherwise told, going to be a change in the schedule. As usual, I worked in the kitchen, finished milking then got supper on the table. Again, I lay two place settings. Dan upon entering the room, repeated yesterday's action removing mine. He looked at the food, plating a portion not enough for a petite model. This was part of the punishment, not enough food. I was angry.

"Dan, stop this crazy crap."

"Boy, don't tell me how to run my house."

Instinctually my stance became aggressive, again calculating my chances of taking him. Fighting would be playing by his rules and winning would mean I'm a murderer. I'm not that person.

He preempted me. "Don't even think about it boy."

One of Dan's initial likable qualities was intuition, now it was a problem.

"I need more food than this," I complained, disgusted at the offering.

Dan looked at the plate, reluctantly doubling the portion, still insufficient in the eyes of almost all nineteen-year olds.

"Boy, you'll be staying until your debt is paid."

"How long will that be?"

"That's up to you boy. Damn site longer with your appetite."

Apart from some bread, and what I scavenged, this was the first real food since that fateful night. I ate like an animal, my mouth close to the plate, shoveling, chewing, and swallowing simultaneously.

No matter how I asked Dan, he wasn't willing to put a timeline on the detention. The pieces of information relayed were the mechanic had taken photographs, and no he wouldn't ask the insurance to pay. They just had a claim, reminding me. I asked for an invoice to see the cost, and he laughed. At night after everything was clean, I was locked in my room like a captive, a slave.

Apart from the locked door and little food, Dan made other changes. I wasn't to get the paper and mail anymore and make enough food for two days. He didn't want me sneaking food as I cooked. "That's the same as stealing," he said.

***

It was still early, casually walking to the front door. "I'm going for a walk," specifically pausing, making sure I looked him in the eye, "And then I am going to bed." Quite clear about the whole thing.

"You're no longer leaving this house at night, once you're in, that's it." His monotone voice fearful and weird.

"I'm not going anywhere, and you know it," proceeding onto the front porch.

"I'm warning you boy." Dan growling.

I was irritated, frustrated. "What the fuck! You know I'm not going anywhere. Where do you think I'm going, home?" Reminding him of how stupid I was, but he didn't need it fully aware of my predicament. "You don't have to be such a fucking ass-hole about it," concluding and turning.

That was the mistake, turning that is, as there is no difference in this situation and turning your back on a wild animal. It was seconds, no time to react in any way. I heard a noise, then a sharp pain in my back and around my throat. Dan sprung from his chair sprinting, body flying, knee directed to the middle of my back. I crumbled to the floor as his arm swept around, melding with my throat. The force of our bodies landing on the wooden deck could have broken my back, neck, God knows.

"I warned you. I always give warnings." Dan's words were deadly.

I couldn't breathe and couldn't answer, only able to splutter hoarse sounds.

"Never understand why they complain." His spit splashing my cheeks.

Dan dragged me by the ankles back into the living room, chin hitting the stoop, and chest beating the floor. My voice box couldn't carry words, only a combination of cries and grunts.

I underestimated Dan's strength. He picked me up like a rag doll, threw me over the side of a chair, commanding me not to move.

Martha's warning was clear. His reactions to everything weren't due to her death, a crazy divorcee, but because this is who he is.

I regained control, said. "It's fine. I'm going to my room, leave me alone for fuck's sake. You could have fucking killed me?"

Quickly Dan responded, "Then why you tempting me boy?

I became truly scared. This was the second off-the-cuff statement, and Dan was taking off his belt.

"What the fuck are you talking about?" backing up, sensing ultimate danger.

Dan's answer was to make a lasso, wrapping the belt around my neck. He was too fast, barely knew what was happening. It must have been Dan's lucky day when I fucked the car up, giving him the perfect excuse to be the person that lurked inside.

"Listen boy, you are going to do everything I say." Dan tightening the belt, pulling like a master training his dog.

"Stop this bull shit. You know I am going to pay you back. Stop this fucking shit."

"Boy, you know there is no cursing in my house." Dan snarled, taken over by a rogue wolf.

I let you a defiant, "Fuck off," regretting it immediately burying his fist in my left kidney, with a force that left a large blue bruise.

149

"You need discipline. I give everyone a warning, even animals. I'm always surprised when animals get it right and humans don't," acting like he was disgusted with my level of intelligence.

Dan dragged me through the kitchen, outside and into the cellar, the sharp pain in my side not subsiding. The first time he took me here the space spoke sadness and sorrow, turning out not to be wrong.

Dan repeated himself, satisfaction in his command. "You're gonna do everything I say?"

I could barely breathe, belt tightening when I couldn't keep up, hands fighting to relieve the pressure. His buckle was odd with a bulge of metal that came inwards, pressing into my larynx, stumbling on the last step, knees collapsing, clutching onto leather to stop from being hung. Hitting the ground, a cloud of dust rose, rows upon rows of dead people, those also murdered

- the only ones allowed to watch, cheered at the beginning of tonight's performance.

"Answer me, boy." Dan loosened the belt around my neck, knowing he was going to find another way to use it.

"Yes." Hoarse but audible.

"Yes, what?"

"Yes, Dan."

Then came the whack, the buckle ripped at my leg, leather making a clapping sound.

"Don't get cheeky, I'll beat ya till blue, warned you on day one. Can't say I didn't…and look at me."

There was only one answer, having worked like a horse all day, had no strength to combat him. "Yes, Sir," looking up.

I couldn't see his face, more his chin, chest, belly, and bulge. Dan's reaction more proof he found violence, and especially strangulation sexual, beginning to think this was another one of his foreplay sequences. "God boy." He gazed and mused slowly releasing his phallus from clothing constraints.

I didn't need to look. I could smell it, organ unwashed, sweaty and salty, bacteria feasting on urine and Cowper's fluid, the pungent aroma reminding me of the filthy bathroom in Charlotte. I felt equally as dirty, like a train station bathroom is the only place I deserved to live.

"Take ya shirt off, boy."

It was only my shirt, and if did as he said, slowly, it would buy time.

"Now ya pants."

"No, why?"

I can't say how he looked, their faces are the same after a while, the expression the same as my fathers, and that, of well another couple of men on another occasion. They were drunk, I was out late and shouldn't have been. As sad it is say, the commonality of offenses among my peer group made it more bearable. We would never say a thing, thin red stripes on guys backs common sights in locker rooms.

The belt whipped across my back squealing like a pig, buckle breaking skin. I thought it was only going to be one lash, but the second cracked, landing near the first, doubling the intensity, skin on fire. Dan threatened, lifting his belt high above his head, buckle swinging like a medieval weapon, obvious anything covered in flesh was going to get ripped to shreds. Kicking off my pants I begged for him not to hurt me anymore, pathetically laying in the dust in overly tight Y fronts.

Dan lifted his leg planting his boot on my chest, moving it down my belly, pressing his rubber soul down, then into my butt crack and higher to knock my balls, harder and harder.

"Aggghhh…stop."

Being ball smashed is like someone digging into your heart, blinding white flashes of pain pops your eyes, starting to cry. Dan smiled as if he just saw a new born baby.

"Come now, boy! Whining like a little pig irritates me." His boot moving to my mouth gently knocking on my teeth, realizing this was another rehearsal. One day he'll be done with fooling around and I'd feel his boot.

151

"Get on your knees boy."

It seemed better than lying on the floor, a position even more vulnerable.

"Take down my pants boy."

I did what he said as the pain was unbearable, and I knew he wasn't finished hurting me.

"Come now boy, don't seem so sad, you like my dick right? Straight boys don't look at a dude's dick after he gets out the shower. You did," chuckles so sinister Machiavelli was put to shame. This pissed me off, as I was nineteen and nothing more than curious.

His jeans sunk around his thighs, making me taking it out, organ orchestrating the situation.

"Open your mouth."

He wanted me to say no, arm rising in strike position, not wanting anything in my throat being hungry, feeling sick and already about to vomit. Nonetheless I parted my lips like a baby waiting for a bottle, had to, the lashes left me with bleeding, stinging wounds.

I couldn't look at it, instead, choosing to stare him in the eye. He clenched his ass muscles, its head danced inches from my mouth. My stomach rumbled, distracting him, smiling. "Are you hungry boy, thirsty?"

"Yes."

"Yes what." This time Dan chose to slap me across the face. "That gonna help you talk, boy."

"Yes, Sir."

He wasn't making me put it in my mouth. Again, clenching ass muscles, penis dancing, eye trying to get my attention. I should have known why. It was just a few droplets at first.

"Come now boy, time to drink."

Unconsciously I closed my mouth, urine splashing my face. With wet skin the slap stung, head twisting to the side. Dan's fingers forced my mouth open, restarting the stream making sure urine hit the back of my mouth, spluttering.

"Now drink boy, swallow." I had no choice. "Good boy!" Dan delighted that I climbed the steep learning curve. "Now here's some more."

After the second gulp I realized how salty Dan's piss was, the waste of whiskey, deep yellow and concentrated. It was the warmth that bothered me.

I took slaps for not swallowing fast enough and forgetting to complete a sentence with 'Sir'. When he asked me how his piss tasted, he made me say, "Very nice Sir', for all the sick fucks who need to know. We have a sick man, with a depraved mind, who's wondering how far he could push his boundaries, expanding rapidly. Martha's death was his Big Bang.

Please not my ass, anything but my ass, but he wasn't saying that. I was also hungry, right?... turning to spread his cheeks. Furry brown tributaries led to a mauve sphincter. "Eat it, boy."

"No."

That was instinctual, not wanting to do it, not completing the thought. He swiveled around, buckle flying like a blood-thirsty metal insect. I tried to defend myself, but he was too fast, striking my upper cheek, latching onto my ear, pain ripped through my head, warm sticky blood trickling down. The next strike was just as fast but moved to fight mode, wrapping around my arm long enough time to grab the belt. It was a brief tug of war, Dan putting an end to it quickly.

"If you don't let go, you're gonna pay bad."

He had a physical advantage, position superior and could start kicking until I took my last breath. I had to let go, releasing my grip was letting go on life. I took two more lashes for crying. This was impossible.

The violence stopped, a sudden silence, staring at each other, both considering our next move.

I was beginning to think my wounds were evidence of an assault but knew the police would laugh. I had been beaten many times, usually quick but couldn't take this anymore, soul crushed. I would conjure a final fight if necessary, but Dan's recent irrationality made it impossible to know when that might be. I had to make sure it wasn't now.

An array of haphazard emotions were thrown at me, ranging from desperation to deadly. Should I satisfy him and then it would be over? I wanted to wake up the next day, get to the old barn, check the bike, and get out of here, not wanting to die in a dusty cellar.

"Okay," I said.

I've done some gross things for survival, licking anal debris remains the worst probably because I had to ingest it. The acrid smell hit me; brown flecks stuck to blond hair around the circumference. That is why I said 'No', so instinctually and loudly.

If Dan was douched and spread on a white towel I'd be interested in an experimental environment. I would want reciprocation, of course. It's primal, for men, often wondering why the standard male greeting isn't a look in the eye, handshake, and a quick sniff of each other's butt.

This is always the unfortunate part of horror, beginning to justify what I was about to do, thinking of anything to explain the persecution. It was my fault, meant to be, written in scripture, fore-told, and fate. I told myself everything.

I spread Dan's butt cheeks spitting on his hole several times before pointing my tongue. His anus stunk, tasting bitter, feeling little grains of waste enter my mouth, tiny shit bombs blowing all olfactory systems.

I was surprised Dan was even into this, and don't think he was really was. We were doing this because he could, wanting to put me in my place and judging by the verbal onslaughts wanted me to confirm who made the rules, time and time again.

"You do Sir."

My stomach hadn't improved, with the likely hood of Dan's turning around to find vomit on his ass increasing, made sense to get him off. I did it, taking long fluid licks enough to distract him while masturbating him. Dan went from hard to solid, testicles tightened, anus contracting around the tip of my tongue, grunts got louder. This was over…for now.

***

Dan unlocked my door the same time every morning, brushing aside him, going to the bathroom. I spent all night thinking about one goal, making it down to the old barn. There was luck on my side. About a dozen apple trees with ripening fruit, were not more than thirty feet from the barn door. If I worked hard, I'd be able to head down when Dan went in for lunch.

It was the same routine, too little food before hitting the coup, cracking three eggs into my mouth trying to solve the protein issue, it wasn't enough. Dan kept his eye on the milk urns, so Bessie helped me, letting me squeeze an extra cup. From the events of the last 24 hours, I don't like warm milk, warm lots of things.

Earlier Dan sat at the table drinking coffee in his not-so-white-anymore shorts. A few hours later I saw him standing in the window, still not dressed. It was time to be in the orchards, heading over to the tractor. If he was still undressed, maybe I could go to the old barn now, only a few minutes on the tractor, another ten in scouting time. He wouldn't notice, needing to take every chance.

At first, focused on my idea couldn't believe what I was hearing, a roar coming from inside the farmhouse. Did the windows shudder? Then again. Dan was shouting, "Boy."

I felt sick, raw eggs and milk curdling in my overly acidic stomach. What did he want? After several minutes he still hadn't stopped ranting, 'Boy, come here!'

Entering the room, I wanted to puke, everything he had done came back, pain, smells. Now this.

"Boy, when did you last do the laundry?"

"I've been busy. You told me to do it at night."

He glanced down, showing miscalculation, not missing an opportunity to rub it in. "I've been locked up at night."

"Do it now."

It continued, for a couple of days with no opportunity to go to the old barn, starting earlier and earlier each day, in the vague possibility of creating enough time. Around eleven there was a diversion, cleaning, chop wood, cooking, more laundry. I remembered there were days when I liked these jobs, even the laundry, recollecting my reaction when first picking-up a pair of his underwear, curiosity taking over, examining them, and breathing in his personal smells. Now I was disgusted, my hatred for him corroding me like the bleach on my hands.

***

It was Thursday. I don't talk unnecessarily.

"Sure as hell a whole lot of fruit wasting out there, last pick up of the week is tomorrow."

Dan immediately suspicious. "What you on about?"

"Out there by the old barn, those apples are practically falling off."

"Why you care?"

"I wanna get out of here, don't I? You want money, don't you?"

"Those apples are sour as ass, pick 'em for church. The ladies will make sauce and pies."

I picked that Friday afternoon, having no idea what Dan was up to. I couldn't get into the old barn without checking on him beforehand. The only way was to fill the trailer with bushels, meaning I would have to store them before coming back. This meant picking at a back-breaking rate, but I could taste freedom, it was in that shed, needing to believe in something.

Driving up the lane Dan was ten yards away, watching me the whole time. I could ignore him or…?

"Hey hitchhiker, want a lift?" I acted like nothing ever happened, broad smile across my face, trying a different approach. "We going to church on Sunday?"

"Yes, we are," pondering my motive.

It was a short ride to the top of the hill, Dan jumping off the tractor, going into the farmhouse, hoping he would want a drink, and leave me be.

After unloading the fruit, I drove back but couldn't see where he was. He was watching that I knew, acting normal, looking briefly up at the farmhouse. The breeze died, no birds chirping. I began a pee, then pretended to need a shit bringing me closer to the old barn. Dan would regret telling me to dump outside, ducking behind a tree before a dash to the old barn, grabbing the door. It didn't swing open, now there was a padlock.

I couldn't linger, depending on the angle could be in plain sight. There was no other entrance and no real windows, only circles nearer the roof line, one on each side. I was stuck, pacing, and looking from the ground upwards in frantic disbelief. This cannot be true, the belly of my world sinking into an abyss, desperately pulling myself back, fighting to find a solution.

Dan had no reason to maintain the old barn, at the rear junk collected damaging some cedar paneling. If I removed enough panels and re-arranged the junk nothing would be noticeable, tossing a metal bed frame, lifting a panel. The rotted wood melted like butter, underneath soft black dirt, exhilarated I worked.

I was under, dirty, but in. Light was limited, cautiously walking to the front. There it was, pressing the tires, flat, trying to turn the pedals with a chain clogged in oil and dirt. It was going to be good enough, needing only a clean, a patch and a pump.

Despite exhilaration and looking at hope, the old barns nightmares were evident. Out the corner of eye that offending object lay there, looking at the mattress and the ensemble of stains, understanding it wasn't only my imagination and they didn't all come from a leaky roof.

Time was running out, knowing enough considered myself lucky getting this far, crawling out. The sunlight blinded me, dashing back to the tree reemerging pulling up my pants.

Picking time is thinking time. It would take about an hour to repair the bike with supplies. If I left at night, must ride fifty miles before out of the Sherriff's jurisdiction, banking his counterparts in neighboring counties have more important work than a boy who damaged a car, and stole a twenty-year old bike.

I'd need water, food, and having no money stealing would add another charge. Dan's leverage on me would seem lame out of the Sherriff's jurisdiction, but stealing was different, meaning inter-county, co-operation, courts and time. There was the possibility of begging at truck stops but that also attracts police attention, something I must avoid.

I was exhausted, the serpent squirming in my head, it was always does when I'm at my weakest. Dan, totally dominant, consumed Jessie in a flesh eating frenzy and long forgotten, rarely entering my thoughts. But there was something new to fill this vacant space, someone kind and warm like a fireplace in the corner of a cold dark room. Wanting to be close to him, a source of heat, love -what was Simon doing now?

Simon was an enigma, very poor, intelligent, and well read, compared to me. I wondered who else he'd been with, and why and how? There were no feelings of jealousy, not like my reaction discovering Dan's boi-nest. If anything, it made me love him more, wanting to protect him from the evil world. If anyone wanted to mess with Simon, they'd have to come through me first.

I froze on the cusp of the living room, shirt and pants dirty. Dan, at the table with a drink and paper did not look-up before entering the bathroom.

Half stripped the door flew open, Dan staring at my clothing on the floor, a cobweb on the shoulder.

"You use the bathroom with the door open," in the same voice. It's from another human. "You can't be trusted."

He seemed not to care, wondering why, then realized, he'd use it at some point.

I'd made food earlier, telling Dan that I'd bring him a plate, settling steaming stew in front of him. He was agitated asking if he needed anything else.

"Sit down boy."

I thought he was being nice. We could eat together like civilized human beings, even though my portion is half the size.

"Thanks, let me get my plate," replying optimistically.

"Sit down!"

He wasn't being nice, controlled fire in his eyes, doing as he said, not looking at him, more signs of Dan's metamorphism.

"Na, chin up boy."

I had to look at him. He wanted me too, but didn't exactly, avoiding direct eye contact.

"Look me in the eyes," doing as he said.

"I'm having trouble keeping you in line boy."

My response was immediate, "I've done nothing wrong."

It was a lie meaning I should hold the stare, but under pressure broke away, a guilty plea.

"You're going watch my lips. Don't take your eyes off them."

Dan spent, *the next thirty minutes*, eating and drinking whiskey in a more than satisfactory manner. He complimented me on the flavors and how I had a talent in the 'culinary arts'. He quipped the food reminded him of a fancy restaurant in Atlanta, chuckling casually before describing the flavors.

My stomach churned with hunger, stomach muscles tightening, waves of pain across my abdomen.

"Sometimes I'm thinkin' your food is better than Martha's," he quipped.

The comments irked me, weird, flat weird, weirder in ways than the crap he pulled in the cellar.

Then he said it. "… and you're not getting any."

How did he know, starving me was worse than any of his other antics? They had a beginning, middle and end, hunger has no ending leaving me irrational. I raised my butt instinctively on the attack. Dan was ahead, changing his knife grip pointing it at my throat.

"Stay out of my barn."

I was scared, pupils shrinking to tiny spots in big wide eyes. Dan realized I got the message withdrawing. I also realized something, Dan couldn't 'kill', his source of income. Nevertheless, it was easy to feel like a mouse being tormented by a cat, the sadism would endure, one day, probably when very drunk, he'll go too far.

With every day that passed, the chances of that happening increased thinking who could help. I couldn't tell my story to the milk guy. He'd say good, you deserve it, now fuck off. The Sheriff and therefore all forms of law enforcement would have no interest, and there was no way I could tell my mother. My father was a ridiculous notion, Jessie would do nothing. I thought about the Pastor, but that slime ball would probably ask what I did, likewise Dr. Strauss and all the ladies who looked me strangely. It wasn't because of who I was, but because of who I am to them, Dan's farmhand, a label.

There was no point going to anyone from Benton, they already knew the whole story, a version happening year after year. I had one possibility.

THERE'S A PROBLEM WITH PUBLIC SPACES

We were late. Martha would have left earlier but wouldn't have drunk a quart for breakfast, before spending half an hour trying to fill a pocket flask. The lot was packed, Dan struggling to squeeze the car into a spot, which wasn't that small. I was amused but Dan got his own back.

"Listen boy! I don't want you talking to the red-head."

My plan was to see if Simon could help. He'd see how much weight I'd lost and show him my scars, not bothering to acknowledge Dan's order. Hopefully, it didn't matter having taken a precaution.

Outside was mayhem, inside was mayhem, everyone working like ants collectively creating a celebration for a forgettable religious event.

Three men were erecting a tent, poles laid out, the canopy on top. Eyes went out for help. Being a beefy guy brings few fortuitous moments, after all most of mother's china was broken by me. They looked expectantly, I hesitated.

"Get a move on, boy." Dan barked.

I grabbed the rope and pulled, tent rising, pairs of boys lining up to place long tables underneath. Simon was one of them, looking at him, instantly feeling bad. He has money and could get me a patch, pump and few dollars for the road. This was good for me, but a bad thing for him. His family could ill afford it, not liking what I must do.

Where has Dan gone? - must be inside, but the threat remained easily able to look out any window. Trying to directly talk to Simon was out. I worked tying the canvas down eyeing Simon, who only looked down. Come on Simon don't you see me?

We were ready, the boys filed in, synchronized they equaled the tables and flipped them. Simon was ten feet away, eyes burning into his body. Briefly he looked up, then down. He had seen me, thank God. No, he was letting me know he saw me, and was keeping his distance.

161

A man ordered the boys to get chairs, reconsidered, telling me and another young guy to join them.

The community space was filled with tables, some for food and some for folks to sit, women busy in the kitchen. No Dan, none of the tier one males present. They must be in the nave.

The small storage room was stacked with chairs. The group mostly younger, and I by far the largest, was told to unstack sets of four chairs and hand them to each boy.

'God' has been a significant waste of time in my life, but couldn't ignore the irony, the church now bringing chances for survival, previously seeing only it as a source of destruction.

Simon was fourth in line, becoming quickly frustrated failing to get his attention. He appeared sullen, before remembering he was specifically not recognizing me. It didn't mean he wasn't acutely aware of my every move, tapping my pocket. Simon flicked his eyelids twice.

When it was his turn, I wanted to slam the door and make love to him. Instead didn't look at him at all, turning my head nonchalantly showing the red mark where Dan's buckle struck, slipping the note into his hand with a stack of chairs.

We were called to service, our pew filled with the usual suspects plus three others, elderly people looked for seats. The Pastor noticing went to his pulpit.

"Excuse me," chatter dying down. "Please can all the young people stand at the back and let folks with tired legs take a seat."

I didn't wait for Dan's approval moving to a back corner, Simon shuffling to the other. Where we were, both of us above average height, had eye contact while making sure Dan's face was forward.

I observed, Simon quietly waiting, just looking straight ahead. It wasn't until after the Pastor finished his opening remarks, he gently nodded three times.

He had read note. My broad smile was hard to control, tears of joy impossible to quell. Simon would help repair the bike, give money and my life begins again. If it wasn't for

Simon I would have deleted this portion of my life a long time ago, pretending the whole fucking nightmare never happened. Simon, my sweet, ginger Jesus.

How was Simon going to give money and when? He waited, the Pastor droned on, Simon scratched his nose. Why with both hands? His fingers making the letter "P", clenching my eyes. If we were caught in the bathrooms, it would be over, someone finding our skeletons while widening the road in a dozen years. Perhaps he didn't mean that, possibly he'd leave money in the bathroom. How and when was he going to get the patch and pump? I needed to speak to him, wondering how long Dan would want to stay after the service, hoping he wouldn't want to run home to re-soak his brain having fuel in his inside pocket.

For the rest of the service I thought of one thing. Daniel Adams is about to make mistakes. Everyone does, basking in glory, knowing my time would come.

When the service was over, I didn't want to move without a command, Dan motioning me over. "You may eat, not much," surveying the swarm heading for refreshment.

One of his farmer buddies tapped him on the shoulder. "I need five minutes with you." He didn't look very happy, prodding knuckles into Dan's ribs.

Realizing he had little option, Dan whispered. "Now I'm gonna trust you, been begging for it. So here it is," grunting, "…and stay within sight!"

I didn't answer, communicating by sight only, suitable method for those that mal treat. Silence speaks volumes in public places.

The ladies paraded, garnished with wide, proud smiles, and checkered aprons delivering dish after dish. A ceremony technically more religious than all the crap I just heard. I salivated, where was Simon?... glancing out the window having a full view of the tent, pleased I was previously cautious.

Simon semi-babysat Stenton's kids. He and the girls weren't quietly sitting in the heat waiting to be baked. He led a simple song, they're hands slapping together to a rhyme, girls giggling. "Again Si."

163

He saw me in the window, looked up, smiling wider. When was I going to see you again?

"What you lookin' at?" The voice could come from anybody, breath and snark gave him away. "Go get ya food, sit at the end of that table."

Dan appeared angry, probably the result of talking to the other farmer. Dan wasn't the most popular guy in town, probably losing some of his cover with Martha's death. What would he be like if at home? …a raging bull, reinforcing urgency, hoping Simon could help me tonight.

I selected cautiously, the queue not knowing what to make of me. What would be better, sweet potatoes or regular potatoes? If only they understood.

Despite my previous antithesis towards God, it was his 'home' which set the scene for more fortune, the Pastor clapping his hands.

"Thanks to all your generous contributions we have these…"

No, not the food, pointing to three window-wall units trying to fight off heat from the kitchen and the blazing sun scorching the roof, cold air circulating. It was significantly hotter outside.

I am a cynic. It adds an underlying layer of possible context, hopefully outrageous spicing it up into the world of humor wondering if the Pastor had a real concern for the elderly, or clearing the youth out was preparation for future paring.

"Once again, could the youngsters use the tent please."

I followed, unnecessary to look at Dan, to happy scene with youth celebrating. Doesn't he realize there are variables in a crowd?

Mr. Stenton's family and Simon were in rapturous laughter, admiring them, confidence in God brought liberation.

"Hey, John come join us." Mr. Stenton reaching out with a wide arm, half hugging, apparently delirious from too much God and loud enough even for Dan to hear.

"Thank you, Mr. Stenton." Not letting down the volume.

He made me take the seat opposite Simon. We sat blank faced for five minutes.

"Why ain't you boy's talking?" Mr. Stenton inquired, "Never get it when young guys don't get along."

There was so much babble, Mr. Stenton's attention already distracted, starting with the obvious stuff. "Did you have a good week?" All loud enough to hear.

I sneaked in, "Can you give it to me know."

"Yes and no."

My expression said, what the fuck! Simon responded.

"It's a bad idea."

Teeth clenched, my floppy tongue in the way, blood oozed, the taste filling my mouth and throat.

"What's a bad idea?" I needed to know.

"I'll still help you."

I have to place faith in him, something I wasn't used to, cutting against the grain of my psychology. Trust and faith are qualities developed from good parenting. I had some in my mother but frequently she didn't deliver, because she couldn't. Its mysterious why my father chose to deny himself one of the greatest feelings a man can have. Being able to provide for his family, seeing the children's faces when their plates are filled, or from the comfort of warm beds. It goes to show how selfish he was.

 Mr. Stenton got up to chase his girls. Mrs. Stenton went inside, handkerchief soaked with sweat.

I tried to ventriloquize. "I need to get out of here."

Simon, with his back to the window didn't have to. "Hide in our old barn."

My expression made it clear what I thought of that.

Simon tried to clarify. "On the roads, they'll pick you up, not just for the fun of it, but because Dan needs you. Your money to him! He will want to get you back."

Simon looked worried, knowing he was right, having the same thought. It was why Dan hadn't taken it all the way, so far. More wanting to play with rather than damage his goods butt that could change in an instant having seen deadly in him. I didn't want to accept Simon's analysis, slowly moving my head to the left then right.

Simon was insistent, getting irritated I didn't understand he was right.

"If the Sherriff gets you, good luck ever getting out of here," words crashing in my head like symbols inches from my ears.

I kept one eye on the window expecting to see Dan. I wasn't scared of his reaction, Mr. Stenton asked me to sit with them and I wasn't 'really' talking to Simon.

He never came, worse, the Sherriff, surveying the scene from the window, disappearing before reappearing, sauntering through the festive crowd. It was scorching, the closer he got, the colder I got. I buffed up, ignoring Simon.

"Hey! it's not that bad in Benton," Silas drooling sarcasm. "Or have you lovebirds had a fight?"

"No Sir, we barely know each other," was probably one of the stupidest things to say.

Silas rocked on his heal and whistled, like that was biggest lie he'd ever heard. "That's not what I am told."

Simon interjected, the eternal diplomat. "We like Benton very much, Sir."

"Well good," running a fat tongue over his top lip, "just remember there are only two strangers around here," identifying Simon and myself with a finger gun. "Kinda means two suspects if something goes wrong."

Simon's eyes popped, head swiveling in my direction.

I did my best. "What's gonna go wrong, Sherriff?"

"I'm just saying, what happens if…," selecting a girl from the crowd inappropriate to describe, "…was found in the woods with her knickers in her mouth."

Simon gulped, I vomited. All the desperately needed nourishment on the grass.

"Eat something bad boy?"

"No, Sir."

The Sherriff wasn't done, placing a strong hand on Simon's shoulder. "No offense son but you're a bend-over-boy. The jury will acquit you."

166

He winked at me, letting me know I'm his man. The guy could be an actor in movies only sick people watch, and always had one last remark.

"You know, I'm gonna see you later," turning with a lascivious smirk.

My belly disappeared sucking down a posit, the remnants of my food, instantly knowing what he meant. My mind was lost, a haze fogging my vision, slowly losing control.

Simon stunned looked at me like an advocate to a client. "I'm still right, they'll find you on that stupid bike. Lay low, when everything settles run at night," he tried to smile when saying, "got $25 when the time comes."

He was brave, breaking his heart as he wouldn't be able to boast about his bonus to his Dad and brothers, before pushing the extra money into his Mother's palm watching her light up. The possibility of a kiss, a hug and the warm feeling of her bosom disappearing.

I barely heard him, trying to shun the Sherriff from my head, not able to think, shaking my head. "No… No… please."

"You don't get it. There's plenty of ways out, but Silas will have them covered for a few days. Hide in our old barn. They'll never look under their noses." Simon said confidently, body language indicating even from a distance we were talking. Out the corner of my eye Dan was there, maybe 40ft away, laughing.

I'd given him another reason to persecute me, starting with making me sit in the rear of the pickup, racing home trying to throw me from side to side. I've been on a few Redneck Rodeos before and knew what to do.

He persisted. "There is no more food for you today." The controlled manner gone, Dan's tone deep and loud, muscles flexed, engorged veins trickled from his temples, brain electrified.

"Why?'

"I gave you a chance. You have an honesty problem," pretending he knew something about the subject.

"No, I don't. What are you talking about?"

"I told you not to speak to ginger-boy. What didn't you understand?"

"Mr. Stenton asked me to sit with them. What was I to do?"

That made him think, returning to the new character he invented for himself, or should I say the character that liked to take over from time to time.

"Doesn't mean you should? It's me you ask," pointing to his chest, pausing, "and why were you *exactly* fucking around in my barn?"

I didn't answer the last time, and wouldn't unless pressed, but now he was and I was angry, wanting this to be over, ready to fight.

"Because that's what you do there...or did." I screamed defiantly, "Said *this* never happens before. Martha warned me about you."

Dan slowed down his reaction indicating that was a revelation but kicked it up a gear to menacing, "You're a cheeky little fuck."

I knew he wanted to hit me and if so would say my piece first.

"...This is Martha's farm, you owe lots of money, may even lose some land, the milking equipment is leased, the car is leased." He was surprised, and I had more. "None even the fucking crate of beer was yours."

"So, fucking what. None of your business" Dan, unimpressed, chuckled as if he had a big surprise.

"I admired you and now," disgusted, flicking my fingers.

"Get this place cleaned up. We're having a visitor tonight and want to eat good," letting out a wry smile. "Tonight, your gonna repeat all that carp with a dick up your ass while I beat the crap out of you."

Variations of Dan had manifested themselves since my arrival. He started out a loving man but with each new incarnation became more dangerous. How dangerous was this version going to be? Considering there will be two, at least twice as dangerous was a fair assumption. Tonight, could be the night they'll go too far. 'Tonight to far, tonight to far', the same sentence repeating itself time and time again.

Dan had done many things and was the kind of man who would continue, if left unchecked. Free from his wife with a victim at his heals, his alcohol influenced, guilt-ridden, out-of-control mind would continue. Was guilt his weak spot? No, he had lived with guilt for a long time, the pleasure he derived from doing bad things greater.

None of this solved my problem, desperately peeling vegetables, cutting meat, clinging onto the knife knowing it could protect me, or use it to end it right now. Cooking the only way I knew how, morsels of creativity keeping me from going crazy and doing something foolish. I gave all my best shots to be rational, knowing I couldn't kill yet had to stay alive.

Manual labor is good for creativity, so is exercise, thinking of some way to slow Dan and I assume Silas down. The pills Doc gave me were meant to calm, convinced they were a kind of tranquilizer. The only problem was, I didn't have them anymore. They were in the bowl on the dresser but disappeared about a week or so ago. Dan again pre-empting a possible thought every persecuted person would have, poison. But I didn't want to poison them, just put them to sleep, enough to give me a head start.

I was done with dinner cleaning the living room, surveying every corner for the little blue pills. The best way to frame it, was in the form of one last shot, a plea.

"Dan, I am being straight about repaying you. There is no question? You cannot do this anymore, please."

Little did I know, they like you to plead, part of their fun the psychiatrists say. So, don't do that!

Dan stripped to his shorts looked like he was ready to go, thankful the Sherriff was joining him, because he wouldn't have restrained himself otherwise, appearing frustrated at having to wait, pouring himself another drink.

'Hey, I'm not being an asshole. I'm gonna start some laundry and I'll bring you some fresh underwear."

My verbiage was planned. I was trying to make him feel guilty that his sadism was unnecessary. I'd have to do this this anyway, wanting to scout his room, as the only reason I had to be in there was laundry.

There wasn't a lot to his bedroom, couldn't be many places, pulling the drawer with his underwear, then another with his T's before looking directly at three little boxes on the chest of drawers. It felt great to manipulate a situation and succeed. Inside the third, was what I was looking for, gathering up his dirty stuff, making my way downstairs.

"Here you go bud," tossing freshies into his lap.

The fact I was being super nice and also showing mal intent missed him for once. As they say once is enough, going into the kitchen hiding the pills for later.

Bending over the laundry basin I felt a grab on my shoulder. Dan did know I was up to something, not what, but quiet as a mouse sneaking-up, wondering if he saw me hide the pills. He looked at the back-door, locking it, key in pocket. Maybe he thought I'd leave the water running and scamper.

"Do that later boy," overly cautionary as if protecting something. "You need to go to your room."

The padlock snapped shut, metal on metal, metal on wood.

The window was small, too small for escape. The only way out was through the front door. Dan had guns in the cabinet next to his chair, doubting if he would use one. The only time I saw him shoot a gun was at a fox, not twenty yards away and he missed. He was a sadist anyway, always imagining my death more complicated, painful and elongated than a mere shot in the chest.

More thoughts pummeled like a bump-stock into a crowded space, bodies of hope blasted away. A pimp beats and maims when sober and kills when high. There was no difference. He was drunk already, knowing this would be the night he'd lose it. He warned me after all, and the reason why I needed to take control now.

"I haven't finished your dinner." Loud but not angry. There was no answer.

"Hey, it's gonna burn, potatoes need mashing." A rumble.

"Come on. I don't want any trouble." Not pleading, business like.

Finally, he opened the door.

"You think I have somewhere to go?" Brushing past him. "Where the fuck you think I'm gonna go?"

***

I heard a car roll up. Details of truly fearful moments are difficult to remember. People remember being scared, never remembering fear itself. Fear partially wipes the memory, a defense against trauma, which unfortunately doesn't entirely work as all the crying and foggy vision remain with details not always the same. I need to stop trying to remember, anyway only had a few decisions left. Where and when? Food or drink?

"You're late," Dan complained.

"Looks like you started without me."

I decided on drink. What would happen if Dan didn't eat his food?

"Sure, as hell felt like! Fed- up with his sassy mouth."

"Where's Chris?" Silas asked?

I had to think for a minute, but the Sherriff jolted my memory to the lanky, boyish doctor who acted superior.

"I don't know, someone had a heart attack. Who cares?" Silas evidently having his own thing going on.

"Shame, kinda like to watch that stuff," Dan reflected. Dr. Strauss apparently another psychopath. They must have known I could hear, it's not like we're living in a brick house.

"Trust me…," Dan gasped like his time had come. "… gonna teach that fucker some lessons tonight."

"Don't do anything to my boy until I'm through with him." Silas barked.

Normally comments like these would send my stomach convulsing, head deep in the sink by now. It didn't because, as I said stopped thinking, stopped caring…stopped everything. I just shivered, sweat running cold from the thought that no outside person, physical or other, will stop what was going to happen.

"I'm hungry and thirsty." Silas called.

Glad to hear that boys! – crushing the pills, instantly worried how I was going to dissolve the powder.

Neither not wanting to, nor should I, look directly at Silas. "What may get you to drink, Sir?

"Whiskey boy… and put some ice in it."

"Fucking waste of good alcohol if you ask me. Pour me one to boy," groaned Dan, liver complaining, that unmistakable sharp pain just under the lower rib.

"Ah shit, you've had enough already, put some ice in his as well. Need to slow you down a bit."

It was confirmed Silas was the boss in their relationship, thankful for it, allowing me to go in the kitchen, and complete my task. It took a long time, little grains clouding the liquid until I tossed in the ice cubes clearing remaining specks.

I presented them with the drinks, purposely not bringing food. They didn't even notice, Silas eager to get things going.

"Take off my boots, boy," he commanded, struggling with laces and swollen sweaty feet.

"Socks as well, I wanna feel the breeze in my toes," beginning with a swig followed by a couple of sips. It was cooler, another late summer storm brewing.

If Silas was married, he'd have cleaner socks. I wasn't surprised, somehow knowing Silas wouldn't have a wife. I couldn't imagine what his aura would do to a woman, ovaries clamping up, refusing to conceive, never wanting to propagate more human horror.

"Massage those toes. We gonna start at the bottom and work up."

Both men found this funny. Toes after ten steamy hours in socks and boots are white, skin like after a long, hot bath, except unclean, rubbing folds infused with dirt, and a stale decaying scent something like death.

"I love this shit," Silas bragging, as if he owned the world.

'Hey! You're hogging the boi!" Dan complained.

"Shut the fuck up, not even your type." The Sherriff wanted to inform. "Your daddy prefers 'em skinny like your buddy."

"That bastard Stenton never lets me fuck his boys." Dan swigged, depressed about his misfortune. "Get me more Whisky."

"Get me one too, but don't be long." Silas winked, unconsciously letting his tongue slip while looking down. How many times did Silas indicate he wasn't the man he pretended to be? Slowly becoming countless.

It didn't take long to put the rest of the blue powder in their drinks, wondering how long the pills will take to work and what would they do?

Even when drunk Dan glanced suspiciously when handing over the drink. The alcohol made him not care, which alcohol does, making it a really, crappy drug. If your gonna take a drug chose one that makes you care, marijuana, falling in love, LSD, art and schrooms. Not ecstasy, nor ice, while making you a loving creature, you're still not caring and there is a difference.

Silas made me pull down his pants, motioning Dan over. "Go for his ass. How many times you said Johnny Boy was asking for it," roaring with laughter.

"God, I hate hairy asses." Dan with another complaint.

"If your ass was cute, like your buddies, he'd have fucked you a long time ago." Silas liked the way he teased me. "Common boy lighten-up."

"Can't I just beat up the mother-fucker." Dan wiping his brow, staggering backwards.

"No, you can't, I want this boy's full attention."

Dan wasn't happy, hearing him grunt, swig, and complain about the ice cubes.

173

Silas needed to make his buddy feel better. "After I'm done, I don't give a shit, just fuck his ass hard."

I worked Silas's calves like he told me to, then his thighs expecting him to become visibly excited, and he did, but the pole in the tent was short. His underwear wasn't stretching, expecting you could fit a circus underneath. The man was huge, expecting similar, not true, fear subsiding.

Horny men are distractible, Silas watched Dan pull down his pants, stopping what I was doing. Dan staggered smashing into a wall, a picture slanting to the side. I wasn't going to say, 'Take off your shoes first', or anything helpful as he continued to struggle with his pants.

"You're a fucking shit buddy. A wasted, mother-fucking, useless ass-hole." Silas spat.

This may seem like a lot of cuss words, but Dan didn't flinch and probably wouldn't have done even if sober. Two good buddies can let out their feelings and all is understood. Who said guys can't express themselves?

Silas wasn't happy with Dan's performance continuing his orders, "Now take down his pants… wanna see that furry butt fucked. I want to hear him squeal."

I was beginning to see why Silas couldn't do that. Dan was well able to hurt me, knowing it'd make him happy if I bled.

Dan staggered again, crashing onto his knees, trying to pull my pants down, my underwear too tight. The Sherriff caching up with me making me massage his groin, intrigued why he was still wearing underwear.

If the Sherriff was that aggressive bull, the public image he presented, we'd be at a very different stage by now. Dan was frustrated, struggling and grunting, his fingers prodding, cotton ripping.

"There ya go buddy," Silas congratulated, his attention turning to me, directing my hands towards his nipples, elongated raspberries, tweaking. Not sure how many time he said "harder".

"Turn this fucker around. Been waiting fucking hours to get my dick sucked." Dan unhappy being a side show, but that is what he was, when Sheriff Silas was around.

Dan tried to focus, his floppy dick waggling not making it into my mouth. This is what you get when you live off a diet of whiskey, whiskey, and more whiskey. I thought I'd be fighting by now, instead I had no more than a prodding finger, followed by a tickle building to lavish licks and a probing, oddly satisfying, tongue tip reaching into my rectum. The dick in front of my face wasn't gonna cum, body supporting it wavering back and forth.

I thought it was a case of drunken men come in two forms, those that cum quick or not at all. Dan was definitely the latter and for Silas it could have been the former, but he wanted more than that. Nothing is really a surprise and wasn't considering all the clues. Silas wasn't married because he had a true love of furry beefy guys, continuing his appraisal of my rear end. Now I get why they were buddies, imaging Dan and Silas camping trip, the occurrence after several days of hiking… all those years ago. It was Silas who spread his legs after night three, too many beers and a dude argument. Maybe that's why he compensated with steroids and being a bully.

It was when he made me move, sinking his body beneath mine in an effort to spread my cheeks, when I saw his penis for the first time. He had kept his boxers on and wondered why, probably he felt embarrassed. There is nothing wrong with a short, stubby penis, I guess. What I didn't notice was the mother-fucker was totally shaved, privates resembling those of a giant baby. I don't understand shaving. Men generally don't mess with themselves.

Silas was distracted, again, mildly entertained at Dan's balancing act. We both saw it coming and simply watched. I for one wasn't gonna do anything and apparently Silas didn't care, or was to chilled, to care. His body was surprisingly rigid when it fell, head making the perfect cracking sound when it hit the mantle, bouncing down, fire-fork barely missing a direct hit on his temple, enough for a blood spew. The sound of his body crashing down was like the last notes of a dramatic opera, the villain slain, my mind standing to ovation as cymbals crashed to a final drum beat.

Dan's cheek puffed on the brick, bruised, his neck seemed twisted, skull bleeding.

"Is he Ok." I questioned, wondering why considering he had gone to great lengths to enslave me.

There was no point, Silas was interested in something else. "Come boy, I want a taste."

Confused initially Silas was quickly aggressive, catching my arm.

"Stand up boi," grabbing my dick sucking on it like a pig, not even a lick first, or a tongue bath for my ball-sack. Nowadays I would slap any cheeky fuck who tried that.

I guess this is where I first got into it, liking the feeling of the Sherriff's waxy bald head and his chin-hair tickling my nuts. I hated him thus happy to thrust all I had into his mouth. The mother-fucker liking every moment, even when I made him gag. However, I wasn't in total control.

"Boi I want a feel that fat fucker in me."

I've only ever seen two other asses up close Dan's and Simon's. Simon's was perfect, Dan's disgusting, and Silas's was weird with pink spare tires around his sphincter, couldn't look. When I entered him, it didn't feel like Simon or Jessie, but like some manufactured fuck-hole, rubbery and overly accommodating. It's the reason why I don't like any man toys.

"Fuck me harder," Silas grabbing his little dick.

The word faggot comes to mind. A word I hate, its hateful, always used in terms of hatred, thus a little virus infecting the vocabularies of the ignorant. The definition of faggot is a homosexual that uses hate on themselves and others to justify their lives, usually miserable trying to score tricks with straight guys. They scorn others for wanting a bit of dick, but it is what they crave with holes used too many times, the owner never caring about the systematic destruction of their body and soul.

I lost it, harder than thrusting, pumping with no mercy. With my girth almost, everyone, male or female, would be crying by now, but the Sherriff merely groaned. Maybe he was used to it, or maybe the pills were working?

"There you go boi." His voice nowhere near resounding, usually a low sonic boom. Silas relaxed, eyes drifting up to the ceiling. It was the latter.

I came, only memorable, because it was the worse fuck of my life, below diseased lot lizards, Silas barely noticed. I saw them for what they were, fallen foe. This, however, is just a round, first four had gone to Dan after all, only a temporary reprieve from defeat allowing time to make decisions.

Dan wasn't dead or dying from my brief observation. As much as I hated him, didn't want him seriously injured, knowing I'd be held responsible in some way. I've heard enough of the sound of metal on metal. To prove that, I moved his head off the cold brick to a pillow untwisting his neck, running into the bathroom getting tape for the gash. The blood, mostly in his hair also trickled down his neck, was now in my hands rushing back to the bathroom washing, scrubbing and rewashing.

I was nervous, desperately nervous while looking at them considering how much time I had. The second bottle was only one third empty and thought of pouring the rest down their gullets.

The question was should I follow Simon's advice and hide or flee, taking the bottle enjoying a long slug. The warmth hit my chest, brain firing up. I wasn't sure yet and took another gulp, then another, bottle almost empty.

I, so fucking foolish, how, why did I end up here? – then in my drunken haze could only think about one thing and looked at the back door, thunder cracked charging into pouring rain.

I thought this was pointless but to make any sense of an escape the old bicycle will have to be gone, staggering from alcohol, mentally someone else and relieved.

I looked at the rotting cedar and with great satisfaction swiveled, releasing the kick on a lifetime, shattering the boards, marching in like the hero rescuing a dame at the end of a movie. The bike wasn't worth it, but it'll be clear I'd taken it, hoping it would signal my method of transportation and that I was far, far away.

I needed to decide, run or hide, remembering Simon's words, 'they'll find you' and 'just for the fun of it' and 'he needs you'. I chose to hide, my brain unable to navigate from the alcohol, and awash with one thought.

***

Bashing God wasn't worthwhile anymore, helping me on more than one occasion. In a fetal position, covered in junk, I prayed for the news to filter through. It didn't take long. The sun was high in the sky, Mr. Stenton marching towards the old barn, burying myself deeper. The door opened, he was armed, scanning for displacement with a flashlight. I didn't dare breath, the door closed. My first reaction was to jump up but couldn't be sure he'd gone, waiting another hour, spending the time thinking why he didn't see me, beginning a long character assessment of Mr. Stenton. He seemed like a good man, even possible he saw something and didn't say anything. Why didn't he physically search the barn knowing there were many hiding places? After a while my brain died like a battery at 10 below zero.

***

It was gone midnight, sky semi-lit by a crescent moon, enough to see while raiding Dan's veg patch picking a few apples. I'd had nothing to eat for over two days, in the last twenty-four hours no water, drinking from the stream. The only noises were trickles and insects. That's all I wanted to hear.

I crept back, stomach rumbling, gurgling, tomatoes, apples, celery extremely unhappy in my stomach.

The old barn backed to prickly bushes. There was a loft area, at the rear a small window far from the ground. The only ground level entrance was the main door. I made sure it was closed, now it was ajar.

I felt lucky having missed another inspection approaching cautiously, then my stomach made a sound enough to wake the dead, the door opened, dashing into darkness.

178

"It's me."

I stumbled out the darkness picking out thorns. It was Simon, my friend, thoughts of him kept me from going insane.

***

Simon, exhausted gasped, "Stenton told 'em you're not on his property."

"But does he know I'm here?" I snapped, post-sex anxiety rising, having taken Simon like a savage, the real possibility of someone hearing us existing.

Simon stared for a few seconds before answering, knowing his response would be real, "I think…Yes…but thinking is not the same as knowing."

"Does that mean I'm safe?"

"No, not yet. They're looking everywhere, telling everyone and bad stuff, give 'em a few days…I gotta go."

"Bad stuff?"

"Property damage, theft."

"I took the old bike to make it seem like I ran, and they wouldn't look here."

Simon sighed, loving me too much to tell me I was an idiot.

I slept better than any baby in the world, satisfying slumber filled with beautiful dreams, Simon in everyone. I awoke because it was cold, rain spatters not ceasing, Fall making its presence known. Drops of water fell on my head, dozing, imagining Simon's body curled inside mine. I was very happy to see him planning a soft and slow sequence for tonight, feeling safe blanketed in warm thoughts. Simon smuggled some food. I was hungry but not starving.

You get used to sounds, the odd animal, a distant truck and I wasn't really listening, head far in the clouds. If they didn't make so much noise I would have been caught. Maybe the wind was blowing in my direction, maybe another kind of force, a loving force, maybe the handler should have told his dog not to bark.

If I ran out, they'd see me, scampering to the loft pushing myself through the small window and lowering myself into thorny bushes, spiking my thighs, arms and face.

179

I ran, just ran, but there was no place to go, the woods weren't big and if I ran into any of the fields everyone will see me. My brain was on fire, thinking of everything, knowing the choices would lead to the dog catching up within minutes and it would be over. He yelped and barked, expecting those sounds to get louder, scampering, dodging more thorn bushes to the pond, a place I knew every inch. My sanctuary and only choice.

Going without oxygen is something I've done. Dan's hands were around my throat for longer than two minutes and when he pinched my carotid artery, on the way to the funeral, my brain was starved of fresh blood. These are macabre examples, but I've spent years lingering in the depths, challenging myself and more prepared than anyone. My scent will lead to the pond and there it will disappear.

I had a strategy, oxygenating my body, waiting for the barks to get louder and when the bushes rustled planned to sink. I kept my head above water long enough to realize the handlers were well behind. I was at the far end the pond, luckily the wind blowing towards me, the Alsatian's teeth gnarling at the other end, the barks diminishing, the dog wandering, sniffing from side to side.

The sight of Silas's shiny head meant I'd seen enough sinking eight feet deep, wind rippling the surface adding a layer of security. The commotion could not go on forever, moving away from any sound. The dog frustrated whined.

I said there was a strategy, hoping the first place they looked were the bushes that created the overhang. They dismissed them after an extensive search and went around to the side where I initially was. Now the green over-hang provided a quiet space for a deep breath. I didn't move listening to them get just as frustrated as the dog.

It was Dan's voice. "I'll get you. You little fuck," blasting the pond. Thank God he was a lousy shot.

Maybe Silas wasn't such a useless cop asking, "Can he swim?"

"Fat fuck swims like an elephant."

Little did he know what a bad analogy that was. Dan, as usual, wasn't done. "I know the little fucker is here somewhere. If we make his fuck boy squeal, he'll come out."

My heart disappeared into a void. No please, it's not his fault.

Dan's rage ripped, bent his knees, flexed his muscles pointing his face to the sky, using all his lungs. "I know you can hear me. Come out or your bitch will suffer."

***

A fire burned, they stoked it and stoked it again, finally satisfied when the flames leapt six feet high. Dan and Silas dragged Simon, half-naked, he wasn't fighting, never that guy. He had said it once, "This is a stain on your soul, not mine."

I am pathetic, helpless and weak not finding it within myself to stand up like a man and say, 'Here I am, leave him alone', because I knew they wouldn't, making me watch Simon suffer before it's my turn. Terrified my heart ached, Simon tried to save me, now he will be sacrificed in their pagan ritual.

Dan pulled out a flaming branch fluttering it in Simon's face, prodding his stomach and groin. Simon screamed, his garments on fire, rolling in dust trying to quell flames. Dan and Silas laughed.

"I know you can see me, boy." Dan howled like a wolf. "No one cares about this fuck piece."

This can't go any longer, feeling like a fraud saying I wanted to protect him, buy him a castle and shoot every fucker that came near- about to get up, hands in the air and shout, "Let him go, it's me you want."

Hopefully I'll get off lightly, returning to my life of slavery. The physical signs of my punishment disappearing with time, but alive. There would another chance, one day, there had to be. That was the conciliatory message I told myself, standing up, raising my hands.

"I care," Mr. Stenton intervening. "I've seen enough. This happened on my land, I will decide."

Dan and Silas waited.

"The boy will get no pay."

It was questionable if Mr. Stenton's decision was better. Simon would probably prefer to suffer the flames rather meet his father's wrath. There would be no point going home, no money was like losing his family. His father would look at his empty hands, beat him, then throw him out.

The Sherriff wasn't pleased when Mr. Stenton extended his statutory rights, rebuking, "I gave this mutt one of his rags. Led us right to your barn. Fuck you!" Silas twisted his body angrily, "could charge you with harboring a fugitive."

"I didn't know he was on my property," Stenton looking blankly.

Thank you, Mr. Stenton for saying that, now I know, you did know.

"I want my boy back." Dan said, Simon wriggling his way from his grip.

"The boy has gone. Of course, he's gone by now." Mr. Stenton said in a calm factual manner about to dismiss the situation, "…and John is not your boy."

Simon ran inside, Dan and Silas stood in silence. Stenton stood steady rifle in hand, but so did Dan and there a faster draw at the Sherriff's hip.

"You should have treated him better." The man with spectacles sparkling in the flames retreated. "Go home."

***

I waited, knowing he would, had to believe he would. Simon was all I had, a person who loved me, unconditionally, from day one.

I felt bad seeing his figure in the moonlight. It was like losing a brother and a lover in one go. We'd make love, I'd take his money and leave, not ready for this final interaction, rushing into his arms. What was going to happen to him after I leave?

I couldn't stop hugging him, crying, tears running freely.

"I'm gonna be Okay," Simon insisted.

I needed to feel it, wanting him to promise. The promise given by a long kiss, our lips touching, comfort, love, not wanting to let this go, yet. I took off his shirt, pulled down his pants, massaging him under soft cloth, looking into his eyes indicating I want this to be special. Simon needed to know how I felt, taking him in my mouth. Simon guided, also wanting my lips on his mouth, before his face went to its favorite place, my fur, mouth moving to my belly, pubic hair and lower. He knelt before me as I did to him looking me in the eyes.

I wanted to say 'I love you' but scared of the phrase, only to find out later, it would have been one of the few times it was true, but overly excited I made him assume the position. His hole waited for me, praising, sniffing, spreading, licking it like the vagina that would yield my children.

Simon made me lie down, knowing this will extend the process, clutching my thighs while leaning back, moving at his pace, pink penis parading on my dark tummy hair. I spat and made my famous fist.

Simon looked down; it wasn't enough. I knew he was right. Simon rode me better than any lady, but he wanted this to end with me being a man.

I turned him over, his face deep in provisional bedding, watching his eyes close as I entered. I could have cum, but to lose this moment was like losing the meaning of life, not prepared for that. This could never be a rush fuck and didn't care if a battalion came wanting to carry me off. I'd finish fucking my friend first.

Simon was a guy that deserved all the affection in the world. I have done many things to show what I felt. Our sex, however, thus far was non-verbal. When he cried sugary happy tears, I cried with him, always tightly holding hands when it was time but needed to say something now.

"Can you come with me?"

"I can't."

I turned him onto his back, wanting to look him in the eyes.

"Why?"

Simon begged me to come closer, having told me his answer, wanting to feel me finish with every possible inch of skin touching. I smothered him with my face, lips, day's old beard, his hands clasping my buttocks, feeling him tightening, me tightening, warm fluid cementing our bodies.

***

"Simon, what's going to happen to you?" My second inquiry.

"Nothing."

He wasn't with me. "No, seriously."

"No, nothing."

My mouth gaped. "Isn't Mr. Stenton going to…?"

"Not pay me! Of course not!" Simon smiled.

"What then?"

"Twenty miles South is a truck stop, someone will give you a lift, travel only by night."

"That means I have to leave now." Astounded at the reality.

"Yes, it does," Simon squeezing his eyes shut, waiting for me to go, wanting to cry alone, believing he's never see me again.

End of Part One.